THE SPINNER AND THE SLIPPER

CAMRYN LOCKHART

ISBN-13: 978-1-942379-12-6

This volume contains works of fiction. Names, characters, incidents, and dialogues are products of the author's imagination and are not to be construed as real. Any resemblance to actual events or persons, living or dead, is entirely coincidental.

Cover and book design by A.E. de Silva

To my lovely mother
who makes books come alive with her accents
and taught me to love a story well told.

PRONUNCIATION GUIDE:

Dienw (dee-en-oo) – Nameless

Diwedd y Stori (dih-weth ih stori) – the end of a story

CHAPTER

I

A Promise and a Vow

The gentle light of sunset fell through the open window to gleam upon her mother's golden head. *Spun gold,* Eliana thought, as she often did when she saw her mother's hair down and loose. Ordinarily the miller's wife kept it carefully tucked away under a cap, so the sight of it was a rare treat enjoyed only by the miller himself and his sweet young daughter.

Now Mother's hair spread across her pillow in a fan of shimmering gold. Yet while those locks gleamed with the very light of life, the pretty face they framed was gray and faded.

"She's not sick," the local physician had whispered

to the miller only a few short hours ago. "She has no fever, no sickness or consumption that I can detect. She is simply . . . fading."

Eliana sat at her mother's side, holding tight to one limp hand. Occasionally she reached out to stroke either one of those lustrous curls or one of those sunken cheeks. Tears stained her face, though she did not cry. She had wept enough, she decided; and if her mother woke just once more before the end, Eliana wanted her to see a cheerful, smiling face, not one red and puffy and full of sorrow.

Mother stirred. Eliana's breath caught in her throat. Father was not here; he had wandered out into the yard, his grief so great that it sent him fleeing from the deathbed of his beloved. Should she call him back? Eliana could not decide, and she feared to leave her mother's side for even a moment. Her grip unconsciously tightened on the thin, wasted fingers she held. "Mother?" she breathed.

A slight line puckered the dying woman's brow. Then, her paper-thin eyelids fluttering gently, she gazed up into the face of her only child.

They were very alike, this mother and daughter, or had been up until now. Oncoming death had robbed the miller's wife of her beauty, sparing only her spun-gold hair. Her features were pinched and strained and gray. But Eliana was blooming into what her mother once had been — lovely and round-eyed, with a dainty mouth eager to smile. Eliana lacked her mother's crowning glory, however; for her hair was an ordinary brown and straight.

Yet, to the miller's wife, this girl was the most beautiful creature in all the worlds.

"My darling," she said, her voice raw in her throat. "I am so sorry to leave you."

"Don't say that, Mother," Eliana replied, scarcely able to force the words around the lump in her throat. "You'll feel better soon, you'll see. The doctor says you aren't even sick!"

"No, I am not sick," her mother replied. "I have never been sick a day in my life. But I cannot live in this world any longer. I must go on to heaven, where I will wait for you. I promise."

Eliana tried to answer, but the tears were rising thick and fast, and she feared they would escape if she spoke. She turned her head away, fighting for control. When she looked at her mother again, she smiled a valiant, determined sort of smile.

The miller's wife, not fooled in the slightest, wished she could do something, anything at all, to ease her daughter's pain. There was little enough she could do now. Except . . . except . . .

"Here, Eliana," she said, and with more strength than she had demonstrated in many days, pulled her hand from the girl's grasp. She held it up so that the simple gold ring shining on her finger momentarily gleamed as brightly as her own hair. "Here, I want you to take this. And my necklace," she added, putting up her other hand to touch the gold chain that lay upon her gaunt chest.

"No, Mother," Eliana replied, shaking her head quickly. "They look so pretty on you. You will want them when you get well."

"They will look better on you," her mother insisted. "And . . . and they will remind you of me. Please, my darling. Please take them. I want to see you wear them, before . . . before . . ."

She could not find the strength to finish the sentence. Tears welled in Eliana's eyes again, but she forced another brilliant smile and, to please her mother, took both the ring and the necklace and put them on.

"There," she said. "See? Do you like how they look

on me?"

"Yes," said the miller's wife. "I like them very much on you."

"Then I will never take them off," Eliana assured her. "Never."

But her mother slowly shook her head. "You must not say that, my dear. They are made of *real* gold. Real gold loses its luster if those who own it cling to it too tightly. You must promise me, if someone asks you for either this ring or this necklace, you will give them what they ask right away, without question. And you will only take them back if they are returned to you just as willingly."

Eliana scarcely heard what her mother said. Why should she care for jewelry now, whether or not it was real gold? The only gold she loved was her mother's spun-gold hair. But the light was fading from it even as the sun set lower beyond the horizon and darkness fell.

"Will you promise me, Eliana?" her mother asked, her voice a faint, whispering breath.

"I promise, Mother," Eliana answered. "Anything you ask. I promise. Only, please . . ."

She did not finish. She saw that, as soon as her promise was spoken, her mother's spirit slipped away from her body, never to return.

Eliana bowed her head and wept now without comfort. But the simple ring on her finger and the delicate chain around her neck glowed bright with the warmth of a mother's love, which lingers on long after death.

Beyond the miller's yard, across the mill stream, safely hidden in the woods, a tall figure stood beneath an oak tree. No one saw him, for no one looked to see him. Even someone looking would spy no more than a flickering shadow and think nothing of it.

He stood still, like a stag scenting the breeze. As the sun set and his own shadow lengthened across the forest floor, his bright green eyes watched the window of the miller's house as though waiting to see something appear there.

Suddenly his gaze quickened with interest. He blinked and seemed to follow the flight of a swift little bird, which darted out of that window and off into the twilit sky. But there was no bird to be seen, at least not by mortal eyes.

The man whispered in a voice like the gentle stirring

of leaves, "She's gone. Poor, dear lady."

A single tear trembled in his eye before falling down his cheek. He was quick to catch it—for it would not do to leave something so priceless lying around in the mortal world. He caught it on his handkerchief, which he tucked away in the breast pocket of his tunic.

Then, on silent feet he glided out from among the trees and over the stream. He navigated around the miller easily enough. The man sat on the bank of the stream, weeping quietly, unaware of his surroundings. The poor mortal had lost his wife, after all. The silent stranger spared him a brief moment of pity.

He slipped across the yard like the shadow of a cloud until he came to the window of the miller's house. He peered inside and saw the body of the miller's wife. How strange she looked to him! So hollow. So empty.

But beside her sat her very likeness in living, human flesh! Dark-haired, certainly, and younger by far. Nevertheless, the resemblance between mother and child was unmistakable, especially now that the daughter stood upon the threshold of womanhood.

The shadow-man's heart went out to the girl as he saw how desolately she cried. He wished he might catch and save her tears even as he had caught his own. But he dared not approach her for fear he might frighten her. And he did not want her to fear him — not in the least.

He spotted the gold ring on her finger and the gold chain about her neck. The sight made him smile, albeit with some sorrow.

"I'll watch over you," he whispered to the maiden, though her ears heard nothing more than the sighing of a breeze through the tall grasses. "I will protect you in honor of your lady mother."

With this vow, he vanished. But not for long.

CHAPTER

2

A New Family

"I will be home soon, I promise you," said the miller to his daughter one day in spring, three years after the death of his wife. "I cannot bear to visit my brother for longer than a week and will return to you within a fortnight. You may rest assured!"

Eliana kissed her father's cheek. She preferred that he not leave, of course. She was not used to staying home alone for such a long period of time. But she was mistress of this humble house, and she knew how to care for the mill, the geese, the pig, and the cow. If she grew lonely, she could always walk down the lane to the village church and say her prayers amongst others.

She held out his hat. "Give my very best to my uncle," she said. With a nod and a smile, her father donned the hat, mounted his donkey, and set off down the road, leaving Eliana behind on the doorstep.

She watched until her father disappeared through the trees. Then, with a sigh, she went about her solitary day, doing her solitary tasks, preparing for a solitary two weeks. First, she decided to chop wood for the fire, then draw water from the well. There were plenty of tasks to keep her busy, and she did not shirk a single one of them. The more she worked, after all, the more time she filled before her father's return.

Since the death of her mother, Eliana and her father had grown close, depending on one another in their grief. For the first few months Eliana had feared the miller would sink so far into despair that he would never recover. However, slowly but surely she had drawn him back into the world of the living, giving him reason to smile again.

Now, though both felt the hole left behind by her mother's death, they got on with their lives well enough. The mill was prosperous, serving to grind the grain of three separate villages, and though they were not rich, Eliana and her father were comfortable in their lot. Sometimes the miller even spoke of adding on to their small house, though Eliana protested that they had no need of more room.

On the third morning Eliana woke to find that one of the geese had broken free of the pen and wandered off into the wood somewhere. With a heavy sigh she set out after it; if she let the fool thing roam free, it might become a feast for some fox. She followed the trail of downy white feathers, calling and clucking to the goose as she went. The whole flock knew her voice and, while not exactly obedient, they would often come to her when she called.

She crossed the mill stream and continued on into the forest. The long shadows cast by the trees never gave her pause. This was *her* forest. She had grown up in it. She knew every deer trail as thoroughly as any merchant knew the cart paths to and from the various towns. Never once in all her days had she felt afraid.

This day, however, something felt different. Perhaps it had to do with the isolation she'd experienced since her father's leaving. Somehow, knowing that no one waited for her back home made the forest itself seem much bigger . . . much more brooding.

"Ho-oh!" She whistled twice, a low and high note. "Ho-oh, here, goose!" she called, but her voice faltered. What was that whisking away behind the oak tree? Was it only her imagination? Or perhaps the shadow of some silent bird wafting between tree limbs?

Giving herself a little shake, she hastened on her way, whistling shrilly. "Ho-oh, here goose! Ho-oh!" She called more loudly now, as if to convince herself that she wasn't afraid. "Where are you, silly bird?"

Something crackled behind her. Something heavy-footed.

Eliana whirled around, her mother's gold necklace swinging free at the suddenness of her movement. Chills crawled up her spine. Her eyes round, she stared into the shadows. But there was nothing to be seen. Not even a little fawn startled into flight. The forest was empty around her.

Suddenly, a noisy honking startled her; but her fears subsided a moment later, for she recognized that raucous voice. "Ho-oh!" she called, turning and hurrying down the deer trail. She found the goose waddling toward her, shaking its little tail and flapping its wings as if trying to fly. It looked spooked, as though it fled from something. Though it was a heavy bird, Eliana knelt and scooped it up into her arms. It nestled there like a lost child relieved to be found at last.

"What frightened you, feather brain?" Eliana asked it, peering around the goose's nuzzling head into the forest beyond. The silent, looming forest, shot through with rays of early morning sun . . .

Some sixth sense told her that *something* was there, but she could not quite see it.

"Come on," she murmured to the bird. "Let's get you home."

She turned and strode swiftly back along the trail, carrying her fat goose. Though her arms were slender, they were strong from hard work, and she did not mind the burden. Having something to hold, something that needed her protection, gave her courage.

She did not see the shadowy figure that appeared from behind the oak tree and watched her walk away.

"She almost saw me," the shadow-man whispered. "Amazing! No mortal eyes could spy me" — he chuckled in disbelief — "but she nearly did. I must take care to keep my distance if I don't want to be found out."

With that he flitted away, and the forest was silent

once more.

As the end of the fortnight drew near, Eliana could not help watching the road with a little more eagerness than usual. She had not been completely solitary during her father's absence, having taken the opportunity to pay calls on neighbors and visit the village church, as was her custom. But the nights were lonely and dark, and she longed to have her father home to fix meals for and to talk with him about the day.

Just two days before Eliana knew she could reasonably expect to see her father home again, Grahame the milkman's lad drove his cart into the mill yard. This appearance was not unusual; Eliana often sold some of their cow's creamy milk to the milkman, and Grahame liked any excuse to pay a call on the miller's daughter. He was a rough-skinned, ill-spoken young fellow, and he certainly would never have dared "speak up" to lovely Eliana. But he liked to sit a few minutes in her presence every so often, enjoying her gentle voice and polite manners.

Eliana, recognizing the bell on the milkman's donkey, stepped out into the yard and shaded her eyes as Grahame drove up. "No milk to sell today," she called out as the cart creaked to a stop. "I needed all of it to churn my butter."

Grahame shrugged at this, quiet as usual. To Eliana's surprise, he reached inside his threadbare jacket and pulled out a letter, which he handed to Eliana without ceremony. He then sat hunched in the driver's seat to see how she reacted.

Eliana blinked several times, turning the missive around in her hands. She recognized her father's scrawling hand, unused to practicing penmanship save in the keeping of ledgers. Why should Father write to her when he was due home soon?

An inexplicable feeling of dread creeping over her, Eliana opened the letter and read it under Grahame's watchful eye. Her face paled. She tried to smile then, but it was a weak attempt.

Grahame, seeing the object of his affections distressed, dug up words from deep inside himself and rumbled, "Be aught amiss?"

"No," Eliana said quickly, glancing up at him and trying to strengthen her smile. "Not at all. My father is . . . he's getting married. He's bringing a new wife home at the end of next week."

Grahame grunted. Realizing that something more was probably required, he pushed out the traditional phrase: "Best wishes."

"Thank you. Yes . . ." Eliana's thoughts whirled. Though she had been lonely only a few minutes before, she suddenly wished she knew of some miraculous word that would send Grahame on his way. She needed no one looking at her as she tried to comprehend this revelation. She needed the creak of the mill, the gurgle of the stream, the sounds of her animals, the wind in the trees . . . and solitude. She needed solitude. But she was too polite to ask Grahame to leave.

The milkman's lad, however, proved himself a little more insightful than one might suppose. He tipped his slouchy hat. "Be on me way, miss," he muttered regretfully. It would be at least a week before his master sent him down to the mill again. But he clucked to his donkey, and the bell on the harness tinkled into motion. Soon enough the tinkling vanished down the tree-shaded road.

Eliana sat down hard on her own doorstep. She read the letter again. *Married.* Yes, she had read that correctly. To some gentleman farmer's widow, fallen on hard times, who needed a man to look after her and her two daughters before ruin set in. "*A rite fine lady,*" her father had written, "*with plesant maners and graces.*"

His spelling was bad, but his excitement was unmistakable. Could it be that her father had . . . fallen in love?

Tears filled Eliana's eyes. She knew they were foolish tears, knew she should not indulge in them. After all, it was three years since Mother died. Why should she feel this resentment at her father? It wasn't as though he had forgotten his first wife! Eliana knew him better than that. He would always love her and mourn her loss, but did that mean he must remain widowed forever?

"Besides," Eliana whispered, "I'll have two sisters. The company will be nice. And . . . and this lady must be lovely if Father wants to marry her on such short acquaintance."

Unconsciously she fingered the gold chain about her neck and rubbed the shiny ring on her finger. Both objects seemed to warm at her touch, and she felt a calm come over her—a calm similar to what she'd experienced whenever, as a child, she ran crying to her mother and was folded into loving arms and held. This feeling was much softer, much fainter, but it sprang from the same source.

Eliana wiped the tears from her face. Her next smile was more sincere than the last one. "I will welcome them with open arms," she determined. She knew that's what her mother would want her to do. "I will welcome them, and I will love them."

So saying, she rose and went about her daily tasks, mentally listing all she should try to do in the week before her father returned with his new bride. As best she could, she suppressed the sorrow creeping up at the prospect of seven more days of isolation. After all, at the end of those seven days she would have a whole new family. Surely that was worth a little extra loneliness?

CHAPTER

3

A Different Kind of Life

In a lonely watchtower in a far-off world, the green-eyed man stood in a large room with tall pillars supporting a heavy ceiling. The floor was polished marble, and atop a pedestal at one end of the chamber, a crystal ball gleamed.

The green-eyed man stared into this crystal's depths, watching the miller's daughter. Watching Eliana.

It was several weeks since he'd last looked in on her quiet mortal life, several weeks since she'd almost spotted him in the forest near her home. His heart still raced when he thought about how close she had come to spying him, and he dared not approach her again anytime soon. But he had a promise to fulfill, so he did not let much time pass without peering in upon her world again.

He now saw her hard at work, cleaning the miller's humble house. She polished and swept and dusted. She cleared out a small storage room, moved her own belongings into it, and then prepared fresh beds in her former bedroom. She spread fresh rushes on the floor and buffed the pots and pans until they shone like silver and gold rather than tin and copper. All this she did with a smile, though the green-eyed man thought perhaps he glimpsed a tear welling in her eye now and then.

Mortal time moves differently than time in the green-eyed man's world. So he watched Eliana over the course of several days, though for him it was merely an hour or two. At last he saw her chopping, mixing, and then sliding a delectable peach cobbler into the stone oven on the hearth. While it baked, she combed out her long, dark hair, arranged it in a pretty crown braid, changed into a fresh apron, and waited near the open front door.

A horse-drawn cart rattled down the forest road,

the miller's donkey tethered and trotting behind it. In the driver's seat sat the miller, whom the green-eyed man recognized at once. Beside him sat a lady of upright bearing and cold beauty, who looked straight ahead and did not smile. Two solemn-eyed girls, neither pretty nor plain, sat in the back on a pile of belongings. None of the party spoke save for the miller himself, who tried now and then to liven up his quiet companions with a cheery word.

The cart pulled into the mill yard, and Eliana hastened through the open door, her smile brave and beautiful. She smiled first for her father, rushing to embrace him even as he swung down from his seat. Then she turned that smile upon the cold woman and upon the two girls, who looked approximately her own age.

"Allow me to present my new wife and your new stepmother," the miller said, leading his daughter around to the other side of the cart where the woman sat stiffly, still staring straight ahead. "Mistress Carlyn, meet my Eliana."

"Welcome home!" Eliana said warmly, reaching out both hands in greeting.

The woman looked down at Eliana for the first

time. Her gaze traveled from the girl's charming face to the gold necklace she wore and then to the gold ring gleaming on her finger.

A slow smile spread across the woman's face, slow because it first had to break through the layers of ice rimming her mouth and eyes. "Eliana," she said. "I am so glad you are my new daughter. I always thought two would not be enough. Now I have three!"

The words were sweet as honey, but the green-eyed man frowned as he heard them. For in that woman's eyes he saw the barely veiled hardness and cruelty.

"My room back home was twice this size. And I didn't have to share."

Bridin, the older of the two sisters, stood in the center of Eliana's former bedchamber, looking around at Eliana's hard work of the last few days without a trace of appreciation in her eyes. She spoke with no malice, but with a sort of hollow emptiness.

The words cut Eliana to the heart. She gulped down resentment, reminding herself that both Bridin and Innis had recently lost not only their father but also their standing as prosperous farmer's daughters in a lively village many miles away.

Immediately after their arrival Eliana had learned (in a quick, whispered conference with the miller) that their father had gotten himself deep into debt and, following his death, his widow had been obliged to sell off nearly everything to satisfy his creditors. As a result, Mistress Carlyn and her daughters were left destitute.

"She married me for security," the miller said with a sad smile. "I know that well enough. But she is a fine woman, and her daughters are good girls. They'll be company for you, Eliana, so you'll not have to be alone next time I travel. And . . . there was no one else to take them in, you know?"

Eliana hated to see the pain in her father's eyes as he made hasty explanations for his actions. She gave him a quick kiss on the cheek. "I am so excited to have sisters!" she said with much more enthusiasm than she felt.

With that, she had returned to her role as hostess, leading the two girls up to their room. But no matter how much she smiled, she could not erase their sad, sad frowns.

"The view is quite lovely from this window!"

Eliana said cheerfully, throwing open the shutters and beckoning for them to join her. Neither Bridin nor Innis moved; clutching their meager satchels of belongings, they stood as though their feet had grown roots.

Realizing that this approach would never do, Eliana gently took the satchels from them and set them on their beds. These were really little more than straw-stuffed mattresses on the floor, but Eliana had covered them with her mother's best, most beautiful quilts and laid sweet-smelling lavender on the pillows. "Come downstairs and have something to eat," she said, taking their hands and leading them from the room.

They made no verbal protest, but both quickly removed their hands from her grasp, clinging to each other instead.

The peach cobbler was hot and aromatic as Eliana served her new family. Mistress Carlyn thanked her but ate only two bites before pointedly laying aside her spoon and placing her hands in her lap. Bridin and Innis said nothing. Bridin sniffed over her serving, whether to keep back tears or in pure disgust, Eliana could not guess. At least Innis ate with some enjoyment if no gratitude.

Eliana took her place beside her father, smiled at

him, and struggled to think of something to say that might break the awkward silence. "How was your journey, Father?" she asked at last.

"Easy enough. Your uncle sends love, of course."

That ended that conversation. Even the miller, ordinarily a talkative, engaging man, felt oppressed by the silence of his new family. He grinned across the table at his new wife, who answered his smile with an icy one of her own.

Eliana tried again. "We may have to add on to the stable," she said. "I'm afraid our donkey may feel a bit cramped sharing."

"Oh, no." The miller shook his head and swallowed a bite of cobbler before continuing, "We cannot possibly afford to keep a horse. I'll ride him into town tomorrow and see what I can get for him. Perhaps," he said, looking round at his new wife and two new daughters, "I'll have enough to buy fabric for new frocks! Pretty things to please my pretty ladies."

Innis sank deeper into her seat and went on eating without a word. Bridin did not look up from her plate but muttered, "We can't even afford a horse?"

Eliana's stomach sank at those words. She knew their house wasn't elegant by any means, but she had never felt dissatisfied with it. How could she possibly learn to understand these girls with finer tastes; how could she possibly make them feel welcome?

She exchanged a glance with her father, and he raised his eyebrows in a sad expression. Suddenly, looking into his face, Eliana felt something she could not quite name. A premonition, perhaps. A strong sense of foreboding, inexplicable and yet undeniable. Her heart began to race, and what little appetite she possessed fled away.

She hastily dropped her gaze to her plate, not wanting her father to read her thoughts in her eyes. After all, there was no reason for her to feel this way! The miller had ridden into town innumerable times before and never come to grief.

Why should she have this terrible suspicion that . . . he wouldn't be coming back?

Chapter

4

Loss

The green-eyed man watched with interest as the mortal hours slipped by. He watched how the two sisters tossed and turned, uncomfortable and unhappy in the room Eliana had so carefully prepared for them. He watched as Eliana herself slept in the small storage room she had turned into her own bedroom, her sleep deep, but her brow wrinkled in concern as though her dreams worried her.

The following morning that worry did not leave her face. This surprised the green-eyed man, since Eliana's nature was ordinarily bright. Was she so distressed by the presence of her new stepmother and stepsisters? Or was it some other concern he sensed in her expression?

The miller prepared the cart horse for his ride into town, and all the ladies of the house gathered on the doorstep to see him off. The two sisters did not look up or offer him even the faintest wave. His new wife gave him a frigid kiss on the cheek, but any residual chill was warmed by the sweet kiss Eliana gave him immediately after.

"Papa," Eliana said, reverting to the name she had called him when she was quite small, "are you sure you must ride into town today?"

"Absolutely!" he replied, pinching her cheek affectionately. "We don't need to feed this great beast any more of the donkey's good meals. Someone will give him an excellent home, and I look forward to bringing back gifts for all of you." His smile included the whole of his family, but only Eliana tried to return it.

As the green-eyed man watched through the crystal, the miller mounted up and set off along the woodland road. His new wife and stepdaughters withdrew into the house without a word, but Eliana remained on the doorstep for some time, watching until long after he had ridden out of her sight.

What could be disturbing her peace so singularly? The green-eyed man wondered. He allowed his gaze to move away from her and to follow her father instead as he traveled through the forest. He sensed no danger near the miller. Could it be that Eliana's senses for such things were stronger than his own?

Her mother, after all, had been highly attuned to unusual perceptions.

The green-eyed man sucked in a quick breath. A premonition—possibly the same one that had disturbed Eliana since the night before—struck him only moments before disaster. He could not act in time even if he wished to.

For a tree branch broke and crashed onto the road just inches in front of the cart horse's nose. The beast screamed and reared up suddenly, and the miller tumbled to the ground.

He struck his head on a stone and lay still.

Blood pooled in a red circle.

Helpless, the green-eyed man watched as the horse turned and bolted up the road, back toward the miller's house. "Eliana!" he whispered, his breath fogging the surface of the crystal ball. "The poor dear girl . . ."

Two days later Eliana found herself walking back from the churchyard, following many paces behind Mistress Carlyn and her daughters. Her heart felt like a stone in her chest, its heaviness so great, she struggled to lift one foot after the other.

Behind her, the miller rested in his new grave beside the grass-grown grave of Eliana's mother. Eliana could only hope that their eternal souls were reunited in heaven even as their mortal remains were reunited here on earth.

Too many thoughts pressed at the gates of her mind, crowding against each other so that none could get through, leaving her in a foggy haze of pure misery. The loss of her mother had been devastating, but the love of her father had supported her through it. But with Papa now lost to her as well, whom could she turn to for comfort?

The three figures ahead of her shed no tears. They exchanged tense whispers, their voices too low for Eliana to overhear, but she knew that they did not mourn the miller's loss. Once more she found herself struggling to stifle resentment. After all, they did not *know* him as she did. Mistress Carlyn had met him only a few weeks earlier, and Bridin and Innis could view him only as the usurper of their own dead father's role. How could they possibly comprehend what his loss truly meant? How could they when they did not love him?

The walk home from the village church was only two miles, but it seemed much longer to Eliana. The forest shadows hung oppressively above her, and the whole world seemed to mock her with sunshine and greenery and flowers. By the time she neared the mill yard, even the familiar sight of the big mill wheel struck her as somehow cruel. How could it go on turning? How could the stream go on flowing when her world had suddenly come to such a crashing halt?

Her stepmother and stepsisters waited for her inside the cottage. Practically strangers. But what could she do? Stand out here in the yard for the rest of the day?

Her fingers moving without conscious thought, Eliana touched her mother's gold necklace and rubbed the dainty gold ring. They seemed to warm under her touch, and with that warmth she felt a sudden glow of love deep down inside her — a mother's love that never dies and never truly goes away.

She knew then what she must do. She must enter her father's house and face those three strangers. She must reach out to them with her heart and love them, her new, strange family. She could not bear to live in a world without love, and if they would not love her . . . well, that was their business. She could only do her own small part.

With this determination bolstering her spirit, Eliana approached the cottage door. But Mistress Carlyn stepped into the opening and blocked her way before she could cross the threshold.

"Eliana," Mistress Carlyn said, her voice freezing the warm summer air before her very lips. "It seems to me that a young girl in mourning should not adorn herself in flashy golden trinkets."

Eliana gaped at her stepmother in surprise. Then she looked down at the ring on her finger and touched again the necklace that lay against her heart. "They were my mother's," she said softly. "I wear them always to remember her by."

Mistress Carlyn's eyes narrowed. She did not need to speak for Eliana to clearly read her expression, which said with more power than mere words: *Why should you have pretty jewelry when all of my own daughters' fine things have been sold away?*

"Take those off at once, Eliana," Mistress Carlyn said, and held out her hand. "Give them to me."

For a terrible moment, anger flared in Eliana's gentle soul. She clutched the necklace tightly, felt the pressure of the ring band about her finger. She wanted to fight, to lash out at this woman who was not her mother, who would never be anything like a mother to her!

But then she recalled her own mother's dear voice: *"Real gold loses its luster if those who own it cling to it too tightly. You must promise me, if someone asks you for either this ring or this necklace, you will give them what they ask right away, without question."*

A sob welled up in Eliana's throat. But she swallowed it down and, without a word, unclasped the necklace and slipped the ring from her finger. She placed both into Mistress Carlyn's outstretched palm.

Her stepmother closed her fingers over them and stepped back into the cottage. As she did not forbid Eliana to follow, Eliana stepped inside, her shoulders hunched, her head bowed. Bridin and Innis sat on low stools near the hearth, their arms wrapped around themselves as though cold, though the day was warm. Mistress Carlyn approached the two girls, and Eliana knew she intended to offer them the gold ornaments as gifts to lighten their spirits.

But even as her stepmother opened her fist, Eliana saw her pause. She lifted first the necklace then the ring up to her face for closer inspection.

Then, much to Eliana's surprise, Mistress Carlyn spat a vicious curse. "Painted!" she said. "Painted clay! Cheap trinkets, not worth a penny."

With this, she flung both of Eliana's treasures into the ashes of the cold fireplace, where they landed in little clouds of dust.

"Come away from there, girls," Mistress Carlyn said roughly to her girls. "Upstairs with both of you. Bridin, I want you to help your sister move her things out of your room and into Eliana's. No child of mine will have to *share* a bedchamber!"

"Where will Eliana sleep?" Innis asked meekly, possibly the first words she had spoken since arriving at the miller's house days ago.

Mistress Carlyn shot Eliana a cold look. "She can sleep in here, close to the hearth. She'll be comfortable enough, I'm sure. It's not as though she is *used* to nice things."

Bridin and Innis exchanged glances. Neither dared look Eliana's way.

At a sharp word from their mother, the two sisters jumped to their feet and hastened up the stairs, and Mistress Carlyn followed close behind to see that they obeyed her properly.

Eliana felt as though the ground gave way beneath her. She half knelt, half fell to the hearthstones, her hands plunging into the gray ashes. One hand found the necklace, the other, after some searching, the ring. She pulled them both out, blowing away the grime and rubbing them on the sleeve of her mourning dress.

Painted clay? Perhaps they were. She saw now, as though for the first time, how chipped the paint was, how ugly they were, when one bothered to notice. *Real gold*, her mother had called them, but perhaps she didn't know what real gold was? Mother wasn't a fine farmer's wife like Mistress Carlyn, after all.

"I don't care," Eliana whispered. She slipped the necklace back around her neck and slid the ring back onto her finger. "They're *real gold* to me."

Her tears fell hot and fast, splashing into the ashes and trailing streaks through the soot on her face.

The green-eyed man blinked several times. What was this strange pricking in his eye? He frowned, shook his head, and put up a finger to catch that which fell down his cheek. A tear? Was it possible that he could actually weep for a *mortal?*

"Whatever have you found that enraptures you so?"

The green-eyed man startled so violently that his tear went flying, crashed to the floor, and split into a million tiny fractals. A shame, truly, for faerie tears are worth more than a kingdom. He turned on heel and drew himself up to smart attention, offering a salute even as Her Sovereign Majesty, Queen Titania of the Faerie Folk glided across the chamber toward him.

She was the most glorious woman imaginable, so beautiful that even the green-eyed man, who had seen her innumerable times, still caught his breath at every new glimpse of her. Each of her movements flowed like a bubbling brook over stones. Her hair was long and luxurious, as golden as a waterfall in the setting sun, and countless wild flowers adorned her head.

"It must be a fair sight indeed," said she, drawing

near to peer into the crystal ball for herself, "for it has held you captive so long that my kingly husband has started asking after you." Her gleaming eyes studied the image revealed of Eliana kneeling in the ashes and weeping into her hands.

Queen Titania frowned, though the crease in her forehead and the downturn of her lips did nothing to mar her perfection. "A mortal?" she said, turning a gaze of compelling inquiry upon the green-eyed man. "What is the meaning of this, good captain?"

The green-eyed man saluted again, his mouth momentarily too dry to speak. "I—I made a promise," he said at last. "A promise to watch over this mortal maiden, to go to her if her life should be imperiled and to intercede as I may."

Titania tilted her head to one side, her golden locks shimmering as they slid over her shoulder. "A promise to whom?"

He hesitated but could not deny his queen. He spoke a name—a name that made his queen suddenly smile.

"Ah!" said she. "Now that is a promise worth keeping." She looked again into the crystal, one exquisite eyebrow rising slowly up her porcelain forehead. "Yet I do not see that this maiden's life is imperiled at the moment. Perhaps not as full of sunshine and sweetness as she would like, but she is in no ready danger. *You*, however" — once more catching the captain's eye — "are at great risk of displeasing your Lord and Master, who has been bellowing for you for quite some time. As you value life and limb, you should make all haste and go to him."

"Of course, Your Majesty," the captain replied. But he could not resist a last lingering glance at the crystal even as he bowed. Loyalty to his master drove him, however, and he hastened from the tower room, taking the steps three at a time in his descent.

Titania watched him go, a variety of expressions playing across her lovely face: curiosity, amusement, intrigue . . . and, finally and most prominently, mischief.

"This," she said to herself, her voice like a cat's velvety purr, "may prove *most* amusing."

CHAPTER

5

A Fateful Boast

"Eliana."

At the sound of her name sharply spoken, Eliana sat upright abruptly in the kitchen garden, both of her hands still full of weeds. Her stepmother stood over her, arrayed in her finest dress — much too fine a dress for the widow of a miller. Eliana had cringed when, three months ago, Mistress Carlyn returned from town and unwrapped this and two similar gowns from paper bundles.

But two years had done nothing to teach Mistress Carlyn any sense of economy. So while Eliana labored to keep the mill working — with the help of Grahame, the milkman's boy, whom she hired to do the muscle work — and scrimped and saved whatever she could, her stepmother and two stepsisters did their best to ignore their reduced circumstances and live the same extravagant lives they had enjoyed back home.

Mistress Carlyn fastened a pearl-headed pin at her shoulder, scarcely looking at Eliana as she spoke. "Bridin, Innis, and I are on our way to visit the vicar's wife. Do see to it that the bread is baked, the hearth swept, and all the other little odds and ends are seen to that need to be seen to. Understand?"

"Yes, Stepmother," Eliana said, wiping sweat from her forehead with a dirty hand, leaving a streak of dark earth across her pale skin.

Mistress Carlyn's lip curled at the sight of the smear. Without another word she walked away, calling out to Bridin and Innis. Grahame led the donkey into the yard, hitched to the same little cart in which Mistress Carlyn and her girls had arrived at the mill two years ago. He assisted Mistress Carlyn into the driver's seat then turned to help the girls. Eliana wondered if he noticed the little smile shy Innis sent his way. If he did, he certainly dared not respond in front of her mother.

The trio drove off down the road. Eliana watched them go, a sigh in her throat. She had never minded hard work. She had worked hard all her life, brought up by both her father and mother to see honor in labor well done. So the fact that Mistress Carlyn ordered her about like a servant, well . . . she could shrug that off easily enough.

It was the constant struggle to keep the mill afloat despite her stepmother's extravagances that left her bone-weary each night when she collapsed on her straw pallet before the fire, shivering beneath a thin blanket.

She looked down at the ring on her finger, so caked in dirt it was almost invisible. Rubbing it clean, she impulsively gave it a kiss and whispered, "Dear God Above, grant me courage! And give me strength."

Mistress Carlyn aspired to better things than the lot life had thrown her. And while there was little enough the widow of a humble miller could grasp, she grasped whatever she could.

So she and her two daughters sat in the parlor of the vicarage, looking down their noses at the other middleclass ladies who inhabited the village. Mistress

Carlyn considered herself superior to these women, but there was no better society to be had for many miles around. So she condescended to be part of this small circle, intimidating the vicar's wife with her coldness.

Bridin and Innis sat quietly on either side of their mother and dared not speak a word.

"My boy Ailbert is back on a visit," said Mrs. Barclay, the draper's wife, smiling round at those in the parlor, though that smile skirted quickly away from Mistress Carlyn's frosty stare. "He works as a stable boy up at Craigbarr," she added with pride.

Everyone murmured approvingly at this, even Mistress Carlyn. Craigbarr was King Hendry's summer palace, some twenty miles away. Even a stable boy who worked there must be afforded some honor.

"Surely young Ailbert must hear interesting news from court?" said the vicar's wife, her eyes shining with dreams of kings, princes, crowns, and jewels — things far removed from her own modest surroundings.

"Oh yes, indeed!" said Mrs. Barclay, nearly spilling her cup of tea in her enthusiasm. "Yes, they say the prince is to choose his bride come the Spring Advent Ball. All of the most eligible young ladies of four kingdoms will be at Craigbarr! Such a glamorous occasion."

The other ladies tittered and chattered enthusiastically, but Mistress Carlyn's mouth hardened into a severe line. All of the most eligible young ladies . . . and yet her own two daughters must sit at home in a miller's cottage, with no better prospects than milk-boys and cobblers for husbands! They were surely the equal of any blue-blooded lady of the realm.

"The Princess of Greer won't be present at the ball, from what my boy tells me," Mrs. Barclay continued. "It is said that she will be wed before the spring is up . . . to a peasant boy, no less!"

"A peasant boy?" exclaimed the vicar's wife. "How on earth is that possible?"

"Oh, the tale our Ailbert relates is wondrous indeed!" said Mrs. Barclay. "Apparently this young lad climbed a magic beanstalk into the upper realms where giants dwell. He returned from that land laden with treasures beyond all measure . . . and rescued the king's own daughter in the process! The King of Greer was so delighted — particularly with the treasures, one must imagine — that he immediately agreed to the princess's request to marry the boy."

More chatter erupted at this tale, much speculation

and curiosity. Mistress Carlyn continued to say nothing until at last, when there was a brief lull in the conversation, she spoke in her iciest voice: "I don't see what is so marvelous about this peasant boy's adventure. Once the treasure is gone, it's gone."

Everyone stopped to look at her, shocked that she had broken her silence. Suddenly she was speaking without realizing what she said: "*My* daughter can spin gold out of straw! How else do you think we can afford to wear these lovely gowns? And she only grows more talented by the day. Now *that* is a skill that will bring in wealth for decades to come!" She sniffed and took a sip of her tea, which had grown quite cold under her breath. "More than a suitable match for any prince," she murmured.

Mrs. Barclay and the vicar's wife exchanged nervous glances, neither one able to think of a response to such an outlandish remark. But wheels were turning already, picking up pace much more quickly than Mistress Carlyn could possibly have imagined.

"*Straw* into *gold!* As I live and breathe, that is what she said."

Young Ailbert looked at his mother with slanted eyes. "I don't believe it," he declared stoutly.

But three days later, when he returned to his work at Craigbarr, he whispered to one of his mates as they brushed down two of the fine carriage horses: "Supposedly she's getting better at it by the day. Soon she'll be able to spin a whole room full of straw at a single sitting!"

"Coo," said his mate, shaking a wondering head as he rubbed down a powerful chestnut shoulder. "A whole room full, you say?"

The head ostler walked by at just that moment and snarled at the two lads: "Are you two lazybones wasting valuable time with idle chitchat?"

"Not chitchat!" young Ailbert protested stoutly. "No, I just heard about this most wonderful lady." And, despite the ostler's forbidding scowl, he poured out his mother's story as best he could remember it . . . possibly with a few embellishments to make it sound more credible.

The ostler listened until the tale was told then smacked the boy upside the head and told him not to dilly-dally over such nonsense. But the story stuck in his head, and by that evening he found himself whispering it to the pretty scullery maid who sometimes brought him nice scraps from the kitchen. She listened with complete attention as he told her of this incredible young country lass, and when he was done, she breathed, "Well, that beats just climbing up beanstalks any day, don't it?"

She returned to her work, the rumor burning on her tongue. Not being a girl given to restraint where gossip was concerned, she told the tale as soon as she could to one of the under-cooks, who in turn passed it on to the head cook.

The head cook, who wanted to impress one of the posh and pretty young footmen, told him the tale the following morning. "I swear upon my mother's head!" said she, raising a solemn hand to her heart as proof of her veracity. "*Straw* into *gold!*"

The junior footman, who desperately wanted to get into the good graces of a formidable under-butler, told him the story only an hour later in an effort to curry favor. The under-butler told him that footmen of *this* household do not waste their superiors' time with unverified country legends. But not fifteen minutes later the under-butler found himself telling the housekeeper, who in turn whispered a few words to the queen.

"*Straw* into *gold?*" said the queen, fanning her face quickly to cool the sudden flush. "You don't say . . ."

Minutes later she burst into King Hendry's office, waving away protesting secretaries and councilmen with an imperious hand. "Hendry!" she declared. "I have something you *must* hear."

With that, she poured out the whole story. King Hendry, seated behind his big desk with lists and legers depicting his kingdom's debt spread before him, his chin resting heavily in his hand, listened. As he listened he sat more and more upright, dropping his hand to the table, lifting his chin so that his beard stuck out almost straight before him.

"Whole *rooms* full of *straw* turned to *gold—overnight!*" said the queen, leaning over the desk, drawing her face as near to her husband's as she could. "Can you even imagine it?"

"It . . . it can't be true," said King Hendry, though his quivering voice betrayed just how much he wanted to believe the tale.

"And why can't it be?" demanded his wife. "Stranger things happen all the time! Would you have believed that beanstalks could grow up into the realm of giants, and that peasant boys could carry off bags of jewels and gold, not to mention rescue princesses out from under giant noses? Yet our own Lord Kester has journeyed to Greer and seen the beanstalk for himself, not to mention the gold coins the size of serving platters!"

King Hendry chewed thoughtfully on the edge of his mustache. Why should Greer have all the luck? Why should an extraordinarily large beanstalk *happen* to grow on *that* side of the border and not *this*? This kingdom had brave peasant boys aplenty, if they were only given a chance!

But then, who needs brave peasant boys when talented country lasses might produce even more impressive results?

"Whole rooms full of straw, you say?" He spoke in an eager whisper.

"Into *gold!*" his wife whispered back. Some things are too important to be spoken out loud.

King Hendry's hand formed into a fist, and he struck the desk before him, pounding right in the center of the most impressive ledger full of debts. "Let's send for her!" he declared. "Let's send for her and see what she can do! If she's as good as her word, she'll marry our boy Ellis and be princess . . . and all she produces will go to the support of her kingdom."

The queen smiled at this, delighted in the prospect of such a bride for her son. A gold-spinning country lass was ever so much better than a beanstalk-climbing peasant boy!

One thought marred her delight, however, and a cloud crept over her brow. "What if," she said, most unwilling to speak the thought aloud but knowing she must, "what if the girl cannot do what is claimed? What if she has misled us all?"

The lines of King Hendry's face deepened into a terrible scowl. "In that case, her life is forfeit," he said. "She'll hang at dawn."

CHAPTER

6

A Royal Summons

Sometimes the green-eyed man found it difficult to slip away from his regular duties and climb the tower stairs for an opportunity to peer into the crystal ball. And every time he did, he felt as though Queen Titania watched him, a certain expression in her gaze that he did not altogether like. Would she tell King Oberon of his captain's interest in a random mortal maiden? If she did, how would the king react?

Nevertheless, whenever he saw an opportunity, the green-eyed man would make his way back to the lonely tower chamber and breathe upon the smooth surface of the crystal ball. He did not have to speak a word; the magic of the crystal reached to his heart and knew upon whom he wished to look.

On this particular day he raced up the tower steps two at a time, driven by an urgency he could not quite name. It wasn't the same as the premonition he had felt just before the death of the miller, but it was similar. The sensation of impending doom had swept over him just as he finished running a patrol about the outer walls of King Oberon's palace, and he had cast aside his helmet and armor, desperate to gaze into the mortal world and learn what had transpired.

He raced to the pedestal and hastily breathed upon the crystal ball. Its surface clouded then cleared, and with its clearing the green-eyed man beheld the familiar landscape of the miller's cottage, the mill, the stream, the forest road.

He gasped in surprise.

Men-at-arms, armored and glittering, marched down that humble road, their impressiveness too big for that small space. He saw swords. He saw lances. He saw a noble messenger with a severe face and a plumed hat. All marched directly for Eliana's home.

"What, by all the Merry Dancers, is the meaning of this?" he whispered.

Mistress Carlyn sat at her window, working a bit of elegant stitching on the edge of a sleeve. She disliked such dainty work but felt it a better use of her time than any other task to which she might turn her hand in the miller's house. After all, the end result would be a fine garment she could wear and pass off as custom-made by a seamstress from town.

Her daughters sat nearby, also working at embroidery, though with less success than their mother. Innis could hardly sit still on a pretty spring morning, constantly looking out the window for a glimpse of milk-boy Grahame in the yard; and Bridin found needlework dull, to say the least. Sometimes Mistress Carlyn suspected they would be happier if she allowed them to pursue the drudgery of cooking, cleaning, and animal tending that was their lowly stepsister's lot! But they knew better than to cross their mother. So they sat hour by hour, working away and never breathing a word.

A strange sound caught Mistress Carlyn's ear. She frowned and looked out the window, laying her work down in her lap. Were those hoofbeats she heard? No, the sound was not quite right, the steady *tramp-tramp-tramp* not in keeping with a horse's uneven gait. What then could it possibly . . .

The messenger appeared through the trees, stepping into the mill yard. Behind him followed a whole troop of ten men-at-arms, glorious in their palace regalia.

Numb confusion struck Mistress Carlyn like a physical blow. Then realization came over her in a rush. Her boast! The thoughtless boast she had made without once considering how far it might spread.

"No," she whispered. "No, it can't be!"

"What is it, Mother?" asked Bridin as both sisters looked up from their work, startled to see the deathly pallor of their mother's face.

Mistress Carlyn did not answer. She sprang to her feet, leaving her fine gown and stitching in a pile on the floor. She was down the stairs within three seconds, then paused at the door to pat her hair into place — one must maintain *some* sense of dignity, after all — before stepping out into the yard.

She stood face-to-face with the impressive messenger in his crimson-plumed hat.

"Mistress Carlyn, Miller's Wife?" that gentleman

demanded.

"I am she," Mistress Carlyn replied and dropped what she hoped was a proper curtsy. Farmer's wives, while superior to the wives of vicars, cobblers, and the like, are not often taught courtly graces, after all.

The messenger held up an impressive document with tiny, illegible handwriting and a huge signature and seal at the bottom. The very sight of it was enough to melt ice-cold Mistress Carlyn's knees into water. "King Hendry, Sovereign Lord and Master of this Realm, has decreed that your daughter who can spin gold from straw must be escorted to Craigbarr Palace to demonstrate her skills."

Mistress Carlyn, ordinarily so frigid, felt a hot flush rush through her bones at these words. "Oh!" she exclaimed, trying to laugh and failing. "Well, this is a bit of a surprise!"

And she thought: *If the king finds out it was all a lie, he will certainly kill whomever I send! I cannot give him Bridin or Innis . . .*

Even as she thought this, she heard the footsteps of her two daughters behind her and saw how the messenger's gaze moved to them, one after the other, wondering which was the maiden he'd been sent to fetch.

"Eliana is out in the mill at the moment," said Mistress Carlyn, the words slipping so naturally from her tongue, she never once thought to second-guess them. "I shall bring her immediately."

Without a word of explanation to either of her own girls, without even another curtsy to the king's man, Mistress Carlyn darted across the yard to the mill and stepped into its musty darkness for perhaps the first time. Eliana and Grahame were hard at work, seeing to the grinding of a batch of grain from the next village over.

Eliana looked up with some surprise when she heard the door open, that surprise redoubling at the sight of Mistress Carlyn. "What is it, Stepmother?" she asked, seeing the expression in that lady's eye but unable to interpret it. "What's wrong?"

"You must come at once," said Mistress Carlyn. "The king's men have come to fetch you."

Eliana stared at her stepmother. At last, unable to believe her own ears, she managed to say, "I beg pardon?"

"Hurry, girl!" Mistress Carlyn cried, stepping forward and catching Eliana by the wrist. Her long fingers were like icicles freezing Eliana's skin. She dragged Eliana from the mill and out into the sunlit yard before the girl could utter a word of protest.

Eliana saw the men-at-arms, saw the brilliantly clothed messenger. Her head whirled with confusion. She must be asleep! She must be dreaming! How could any of this possibly be real?

"This is the young maiden? Your daughter?" said the messenger, looking Eliana up and down, noting the difference in her grimy, bedraggled state and the poor quality of her clothes compared to the clean, neat garments worn by Bridin, Innis, and their mother.

"She is indeed," said Mistress Carlyn, smiling brilliantly, her fingers still latched painfully upon Eliana's wrist. "She was just hard at work inside, improving her craft. She is most eager to demonstrate her skills before the king."

"What?" Eliana cried. "Stepmother, what do you mean?"

Mistress Carlyn offered no reply, merely pushing Eliana before her to stand in front of the messenger. Eliana stared at the man, stared at the red plume of his hat. She tried to remember how to curtsy, but her own legs would not obey her.

"Come along, my girl," said the messenger, taking her by the arm. "We haven't got all day."

"Please!" Eliana choked, casting a desperate look back over her shoulder. Mistress Carlyn stood with a face like stone, Bridin and Innis framing her, their expressions much more distraught. Grahame appeared in the doorway of the mill and stood thunderstruck and unmoving. Eliana saw no help anywhere. "Please, what is going on?"

The messenger did not answer. He pushed her to stand in the center of the ten men-at-arms. They set off marching, and Eliana was obliged to trot in order to keep pace. She wasn't even wearing her one pair of shoes! Her bare feet struck the dirt road in a pace almost as quick as the beating of her own terrified heart. Her only comfort was that this must, simply *must* be nothing more than a strange dream!

She clenched her hand into a fist, rubbing her thumb against her mother's gold ring. With her other hand she touched the gold necklace. But for once, neither could give her any comfort.

CHAPTER

7

Real Gold

The king's men did not make Eliana walk the full twenty miles to Craigbarr. In the nearest town—the very town where all Eliana's friends and acquaintances lived, the town where she attended services at the little church each Sunday—a cart was found, and she was loaded into the back of it like some prisoner. This was almost worse than being surrounded by the men-at-arms. At least when marching in their number she could hide herself behind their armor and lances.

In the cart she felt horribly exposed. Every one of her neighbors flocked to their windows and gates, gawping at her, whispering, some few daring to call out to her. She could not look at them, could not summon a voice to answer. What answer would she give anyway?

What in heaven's name had she *done?*

This question rattled round in her head, jarring along with every rut and bump in the long road to the king's palace. She was no closer to an answer when they stopped for the night at a humble inn and she was locked in a lonely, cold room to herself. She was no closer to an answer the next morning when, shivering, she was loaded back into the cart and driven on into unfamiliar countryside, farther from home than she had ever been.

And she was no closer to an answer when she saw the king's city spread out before her and beheld the amazing high rooftops and glittering gable windows of Craigbarr itself. This sight was too much for her, and she hid her face in her hands as though she could hide herself from the curious stares of the city folk who watched with interest as the cart rolled down the center street. She wondered . . . did *they* know why the king had sent armed men to fetch her from her home?

The cart lurched to a halt. "Open in the name of the king!" the voice of the messenger boomed.

Eliana dropped her hands from her face, looking

up in time to see the great, wide palace gates swing open like the jaws of a beast ready to swallow her alive. The cart surged into motion again, and Eliana grasped its railing to keep from falling over, her fingers white-knuckled with terror. They passed into a tremendous courtyard, and vague impressions of marble grandeur and glorious paving stones plucked at Eliana's senses.

But her gaze fixed on one thing only: the wooden scaffold, half built, standing in the center of that yard. Laborers pounded away with hammers and nails, and even as Eliana watched, the gallows post was set into place.

Her blood turned to ice in her veins.

After that, the world seemed to collapse upon itself in a hazy horror. Too dizzy to take in her surroundings, too numb to understand what had happened, Eliana felt strong hands grasp her upper arms and drag her down from the cart. Perhaps she fainted, though no peaceful oblivion of darkness enveloped her.

Instead, it was as though her conscious awareness simply blacked out until she found herself inside the palace, but in a room unlike anything she would have expected to find within the walls of beautiful Craigbarr. It was low-ceilinged and bare, with only a single window. Its only furnishing was a spinning wheel, which stood in the very center. Piled around it were numerous bales of straw.

For some reason this sight, even more than the scaffold, filled Eliana with dread. She feared her heart had ceased to beat, and some moments passed before she realized that the men-at-arms had left her alone in the room.

"So you're here," said a strange voice. Not a particularly loud voice, but it bore that certain quality that fills the room and obliges all hearers to turn to it with attention. Elaina turned now and beheld a face she inexplicably recognized. After blinking three times she realized why she recognized it—it was the same face she had seen printed on copper coins for as long as she could remember. That beard, that long mustache, that brow—all were unmistakable.

She stood in the presence of the king!

In her effort to curtsy, she fell to her knees and could not find the strength to stand up again.

King Hendry looked upon the girl before him with her dirty clothes and loose, messy hair, her bare feet, her dirty fingers. If *this* wasn't a proper peasant maiden, he didn't know what was! Surely she *must* be possessed of magical powers, because that's how these things worked. At least that's how these things worked in Greer, and if they could work so nicely in Greer, well, so help him . . .

"Your mother boasted of your impressive skills," he said, scowling down at the trembling girl, his arms folded over his chest, "and report of you reached my ear. The time has come to prove your mettle. Spin these bales of straw into gold by tomorrow morning. If you do not, you will die for your mother's lie."

Eliana's eyes opened so wide, they took up most of her face. She stared at the king, her mouth opening and closing wordlessly.

He saw the horror in her face, and a terrible suspicion rooted in his stomach: suspicion that he had been foolish to believe these rumors. Suspicion that he had been wrong to make such an implacable decree. Suspicion that he would only embarrass himself and needlessly end this innocent maiden's life.

But he hardened himself against these thoughts, blocking them out like enemies at the gate. "You know what you must do," he said, and backed out of the room. The door slammed shut.

Eliana bowed her head and sobbed.

At some point in the afternoon, Eliana fell asleep. The sheer exhaustion of her own terror overwhelmed her, and she put her head down on one of the straw bales, oblivious to the tickling and prickling of the coarse grasses, and lost herself to troubling dreams.

She woke with a start and a gasp. Through the one window she saw stars and realized that she had slept well into the evening. Her face was swollen and puffy from weeping, and the sleep had not brought her rest.

Rising stiffly, she made her way to the window, kicking straw with her bare feet with each step. She peered out, hoping for some glimpse of the country beyond the palace walls, beyond the city. Some glimpse of land she recognized, some hint of home.

Instead, she saw the gallows standing ready in the courtyard below.

She gasped and drew back, tears filling her eyes once more. She looked round at the spinning wheel. What was it the king had said? *Straw* into *gold?*

"Stepmother, what have you done?" she whispered. How could Mistress Carlyn have made such a ridiculous boast? And how could the king have heard about it, much less believed it? She closed her eyes, struggling to fight the tide of fear and nausea welling up inside her.

"Maiden, why do you weep?"

Eliana whirled around, her heart leaping to her throat. Her widened eyes saw a shadow in the corner, but it was too dark to see more than an impression. "Who's there?" she demanded.

Suddenly the starlight seemed to brighten until the room was filled with silvery light as brilliant as day. Eliana clearly beheld a lean, strong man wearing clothes unlike anything she had ever before seen, as if the browns and greens of a forest had been woven together into cloth. But what struck Eliana more profoundly than his attire were his brilliant, spring-green eyes.

"You're too pretty to be crying," the stranger said, smiling gently. "I always thought King Hendry a fool, but I did not think he was cruel."

Everything about this man was too strange. Too bizarre and too otherworldly. Eliana, instantly wary, demanded, "Who are you?"

"You have soot on your face," he said instead of answering.

Despite herself, Eliana's hand flew to her cheek and rubbed hard, smearing tears and soot together.

"That only made it worse." The green-eyed stranger chuckled. He stepped from his corner, approaching her slowly, his hands held out as though to soothe a frightened doe. "So tell me, why are you crying?"

This must be a dream, Eliana told herself. *All of it. Everything since yesterday morning. And this is merely the strangest part of the dream yet, and I'll wake up from it soon.*

With this thought firmly in mind, she decided she might as well answer as not. "My stepmother boasted that I can spin straw into gold," she said. "Somehow it reached the ear of the king, and now he expects me to prove myself."

"Can you?" asked the stranger, though something in his eye told her that he already knew the answer.

"What sort of question is that?" she answered, her voice sharp with frustration. She shook her head vigorously. "Of course not! No one can! It's the silly wish of a greedy woman who always wants more than she can have."

"So why did she send you here? If these are the garments you came in, she did not have the foresight to dress you well for visiting the king."

Eliana, suddenly weak, sat down heavily on the nearest straw bale. "She probably meant one of her other daughters when she invented the story," she said with a shaky sigh. "But the king will kill me when he learns it was all a lie, and she did not want her own blood to die."

The stranger clicked his tongue and sat down beside her, his hands on his knees. "That is harsh indeed. So this is the reason for your sorry weeping?"

"Yes," said Eliana, frowning and suddenly defensive. "Isn't it reason enough?"

"Calm down, lass! No need to fuss. What if I told you that *I* can spin straw into gold?"

Eliana laughed bitterly. This dream was too ridiculous for words! "I'd call you a rotten liar."

The man smiled and gave her a friendly nudge on the shoulder. "And you'd be right to do so if I were a normal man. But I am a faerie."

She jerked away from him, almost falling from the straw bale in her haste. Suddenly she knew—she *knew*—that this was no dream. It couldn't be. Because there was something altogether too *real* about this stranger's unreal-ness, about the brilliant starlight and the green of his eyes. As though everything else she had always known were the dream, and this, *this*, weird though it might be, were the reality always just beyond the edge of her understanding.

A faerie? She should disbelieve his claim. Yet she could not find the will to do so.

"What do you want with me?" Stories about faerie-folk came back to her, stories of how they snatched children from the cradle and stole young women away in the night.

The faerie looked hurt. "I simply do not want to see you cry," he said. "And it seems a shame to let you die because of a simple misunderstanding."

"Why should you care?" Eliana got to her feet and crossed to the opposite side of the room, on the far side of the spinning wheel. "I'm not of your kind."

"Ah, but your mother was."

Eliana's heart froze in her breast. Her mother? A . . . *faerie*?

Understanding fell upon her in a tremendous rush like the force of a waterfall. Of course she was! How could her mother, her beautiful, lovely, beloved mother, be anything less? Her mother, who was always just a little too wonderful for this world.

Nevertheless, Eliana whispered, "You speak truly?"

The faerie nodded slowly, leaning forward to rest his elbows on his knees. "She could not live long in your world, breathing your mortal air. She knew it would kill her to remain, but she could not bear to leave you or your father, not even for a day. So she stayed as long as she could, until her faerie magic was at last all used up." He bowed his head briefly, as though overwhelmed by sudden sorrow. That sorrow still shone in his eyes when he looked up at Eliana again. "Just before she passed away she asked me to look after you. Somehow she knew that some danger would come upon you, and she asked me to protect you when it happened. She could not tell me more, but . . ." His mouth twisted in a half-smile. "I think she may have guessed something like this would happen. She was always sensitive to premonitions and the like."

His expression grew very serious then. "It is against our King's law for a faerie to let himself be seen by a mortal. I'm breaking a lot of rules simply by talking to you right now."

Eliana, her mind awhirl with all these new thoughts and ideas, found another straw bale and slowly sank down onto it. Her hand moved to her mother's necklace, fingering the little chain links. She felt the gold metal warm beneath her touch.

The faerie stood and crossed over to her. She did not move at his approach but sat very still even as he knelt before her. "A lovely necklace," he said. "Very beautiful indeed."

"It . . . was my mother's," Eliana whispered.

"May I have it?"

Eliana stared at him. She couldn't bring herself to answer, but her hand closed unconsciously over the necklace, holding on as though holding on to life itself.

"You must promise me, if someone asks you for either this ring or this necklace, you will give them what they ask right away, without question."

He waited quietly, one hand outstretched, palm up. How badly she wanted to refuse him! But that would mean gainsaying her mother's final wish. Was she so determined to hold on to her possessions that she would dishonor her mother's memory?

Very quietly, scarcely breathing, she slipped the necklace from around her neck. Slowly she dropped it in coils into the palm of the faerie's hand. "It's only painted clay," she whispered, almost in apology.

But even as she spoke, a change came over the necklace. As it fell into the faerie's hand, the chipped gold paint renewed and began to glow like a handful of sunlight made solid. Eliana gasped, both frightened and delighted at the same time.

"It's *real* gold," said the faerie, smiling at her once more. "Real *faerie* gold. And because you gave it to me willingly, I can use the magic of this gift to spin straw into more gold for you. This I promise, sweet Eliana."

With that, he stood and moved to the spinning wheel, his every movement graceful and confident. He called back over his shoulder. "You might as well shut those pretty eyes of yours and get some rest. This is going to take all night."

Eliana did not want to sleep. She wanted to watch what he did, wanted to observe this strange magic of his. But even as the faerie's foot pressed the treadle, even as the wheel began to spin, even as he took up the first handful of straw, Eliana felt exhaustion overwhelm her. She sank slowly to the floor with her cheek resting on her arm. As she fell into a sleep much deeper and more refreshing than any she'd known since her mother's death, she wondered how he had learned her name. But sleep took her for the night, and she all but forgot to ask him.

The faerie's deep, melodious voice sang in her dreams:

> *"Round about, round about,*
>
> *Lo and behold!*
>
> *Reel away, reel away,*
>
> *Straw into gold!"*

CHAPTER
8

Rising Tensions

The sun rose. The castle began to stir and wake.

Eliana's eyes opened slowly, unwillingly. She had enjoyed such a beautiful sleep, it was difficult to return to the waking world.

The moment her lashes raised, she was obliged to shut them as a blinding glare filled her vision. She sat up, rubbing her eyes, and slowly opened them again.

Sunlight poured through the window, gleaming brilliantly upon three neat piles of coiled, spun gold.

Before Eliana could even react, the door to the lonely chamber opened with a loud creak and a crash. King Hendry's imposing figure stood in the doorway, and behind him a woman so beautifully dressed that Eliana knew she must be the queen stood on tiptoe to peer over her husband's shoulder. She let out a delighted cry and grabbed his arm in girlish delight. "See? See? I *told* you!" she exclaimed.

King Hendry stared into the room, his face full of the glow of newly spun gold. "You've done it, girl!" he breathed, his voice almost lost in his own overwhelming wonder. "You've really spun straw into gold!"

"She's a treasure! A royal *treasure!*" exclaimed the queen. She pushed past her husband into the room, darted across to the gold piles, plunged her hands in, and lifted gleaming strands of thread as delicate as silk and yet heavy like gold. She gasped in surprise at the weight then laughed and wrapped several strands around her wrist as long, looping bangles. "Darling!" she cried, whirling to face her husband, her cheeks flushed and her eyes brilliant with gold thrill. "We simply *must* present her at court!"

Eliana, who had not yet even managed to pull herself to her feet, felt her heart plummet at this exclamation. The very idea was almost as dreadful to her as the gallows waiting in the courtyard down below.

King Hendry gave her a once over, one gray eyebrow lifting slowly. "Her appearance is not exactly court-worthy," he said. "Most unsavory. Perhaps tomorrow, when your seamstresses have had time to make her some proper clothes."

The queen did not protest, for she was too caught up in trying to braid three strands of gold into a woven chain, laughing like a child with greedy delight. Observing his wife, King Hendry suddenly lit up with inspiration. He addressed himself to Eliana once more. "I'm afraid your presentation will have to wait until tomorrow. But never fear! I'll have a bed and soft blankets and a pillow sent in, so that you may get some proper rest. And then . . ."

He smiled. It wasn't at all a pleasant expression. "You would not mind doing it again, would you, lass?"

"And what exactly do you think you are doing?"

A terrible thrill ran up the green-eyed man's spine, and he turned swiftly around, tearing his gaze away from the crystal ball to see the broad, imposing figure of King Oberon standing at the other end of the pillared room.

The king wore magnificent emerald robes that swept the floor with the *shushing* sound of wind in summer trees as he walked, closing the distance between himself and his captain. He was as beautiful as his wife, but more dreadful, more warlike, with a dark brow and darker eyes. Those dark eyes fixed upon the crystal ball. The green-eyed man made a half-hearted attempt to hide it with his body, but King Oberon swept him aside and peered intently into its depths.

"So *this* is what has distracted you from your duties?" the king said, his voice as rich as black velvet but not so soft. "A mortal maid!"

"I am not on duty at present, Your Majesty," the green-eyed man said, offering a humble bow.

King Oberon shot him a quick glare then turned his attention back to the image in the crystal ball. It revealed Eliana, looking poor in her peasant rags as she knelt on the floor before the mortal king and queen, surrounded by golden work of the faerie's hand. Yet despite her dowdy clothing and dirty face, there was something about her face . . . something that struck even King Oberon. The green-eyed faerie saw Oberon's expression momentarily shift, creasing with confusion.

Oberon shook this away, however, and turned

from the crystal, folding his powerful arms over his chest, his long sleeves draping almost to the floor. "You have other duties, I am sure."

"Not at the present moment," the faerie captain replied, his voice quiet and firm. "Nothing more pressing than this duty. I made a promise, a solemn oath, to protect this maiden from all harm. And she is still in danger. You see, she is—"

"I don't care to hear the troubles of a mortal," King Oberon said, holding up a warning hand. He nodded at the crystal. "I see the work of your talented hand, all of that gold-spun straw. Certainly that bounty should buy the girl's safety. You have more than fulfilled any vow you may have made. It's time you got back to your real work."

"And would you value a captain who only half fulfills his word?"

The voice speaking was like springtime itself, and the room filled suddenly with all the perfumes of a blooming garden. Both king and captain turned to see the lithe and graceful form of Titania standing in the doorway, one arm draped against the doorpost, her golden hair shining. She said nothing more. She did not need to. Her jewel-like eyes pierced the distance between herself and her lordly husband, and the two wills clashed in a struggle so brief and yet so dangerous that even the brave faerie captain felt himself shrinking away from them.

Oberon looked away first. The scowl he then fixed upon his captain was dreadful indeed. "You may have one night and no more!" he growled. With that, he stormed from the room, brushing past his wife without a word.

Titania remained in the doorway, smiling softly. She caught the captain's eye, and her expression was so knowing that the green-eyed faerie blushed and looked quickly away.

CHAPTER

9

Tears into Glass

Servants brought in a bed, as promised. Six men followed behind, lugging huge bales of straw. These they piled up around the spinning wheel in exchange for the gold thread, which they carried out with them, then shut the chamber door firmly without speaking so much as a word to Eliana. The chamber was darker without the glow from the faerie gold.

Eliana stared at the six bales. Despair settled down over her shoulders once more. Too tired to stand, she sat on the edge of the bed, holding herself very still, telling herself to be strong.

But she couldn't help it. The tears came, and she

buried her face in her pillow.

Now what? What could she possibly do? The faerie had helped her, but to what end? If King Hendry kept asking her to spin more gold, could she really expect such supernatural aid to come to her again and again? Was she expected to do this for the rest of her life? She would swiftly run out of gifts to offer in exchange for the magic!

The day dragged on. At one point in the afternoon, the queen's own bevy of seamstresses came into the room to take Eliana's measurements. They left without speaking, though casting several curious glances at the untouched bales of straw. Guards stood watch outside the door. Eliana knew this because they kept banging their lances against the floor and talking to each other in deep murmuring voices. Apparently the king didn't want his "treasure" to escape.

At last Eliana fell asleep on her bed, clutching her pillow to her chest, a frown etched into her face. She did not wake until moonrise, opening her eyes to see the pale silvery gleam falling through the lonely window.

Suddenly, however, the silvery gleam wasn't just moonlight. It was a swirl of light there in the room itself, sprouting up from the floor. In the center of the swirl stood a form, and that form materialized into the dark-haired stranger. He blinked his startling green eyes several times before his gaze cleared and fixed upon Eliana where she sat upright in her bed.

Eliana could not help herself. At the sight of her rescuer from the previous night, she burst into tears.

"Oh dear!" cried the faerie. "Is the sight of me as dreadful as all that?" His voice held laughter, however, and he stepped across to kneel before her, fetching a handkerchief from his pocket. Very gently he wiped the tears from her cheeks, taking care not to miss a single one.

"You came back!" Eliana choked, embarrassed but unable to stop her tears quite yet. "I didn't think you would."

"Of course I did," he replied, smiling up at her. "I got you into this mess, didn't I? I proved your skill to the king, and now he'll want more proof, naturally. I can't very well abandon you. How would that fulfill my vow to your mother?"

Eliana sniffed and blinked very hard, finally managing to stop her tears. She smiled weakly but with deep sincerity and whispered a heartfelt "Thank you."

He did not answer right away, merely gazing at her with a strange expression on his beautiful face. Then he shook his head carelessly, brushing her cheek with his knuckle. "None of that now!" He folded the dampened handkerchief and tucked it away inside his tunic. "Let's see about this monstrous pile of straw."

Eliana watched the faerie as he got up, adjusted the position of the spinning wheel, then settled himself upon the low stool with a nod of satisfaction. But then he sprang up again and eyed the bales of straw, considering, his lips pursed.

"What's wrong?" Eliana asked, rising from the bed.

He looked up at her. "Dear Eliana, may I have your ring?"

She'd known he must ask, of course. Had he not explained last night that without a willing gift he could not perform the magic? Yet the asking struck her to the heart. Her necklace was already gone, and she felt the lack of it sorely, missing the weight of it around her neck and against her heart. The little gold ring was her last token from her mother, her last link to that one she loved so dearly and missed so desperately. All of her world was lost to her—her father, the mill, her friends and neighbors. Must this last, very small item go as well?

But was it worth her life? And was it worth breaking her promise to Mother?

Silently she slipped it from her finger, crossed to the green-eyed man, and pressed it into his outstretched palm. His fingers closed upon hers for a moment, and so they stood, both of them holding the gold ring. Her breath caught in her throat, and she feared that she would disgrace herself with more tears.

"Thank you," he said at last and released her hand.

The ring vanished into the front of his tunic along with the handkerchief. The green-eyed faerie turned to his work, taking a handful of straw from the nearest bale as he settled back on the stool. "Would you like to help me?" he asked.

"Help you?"

"Yes. This will take a bit longer than last night's trick. Your King Hendry's greed has only grown! Another set of hands would be much appreciated."

Eager to be of use, Eliana agreed. She handed the green-eyed man handfuls of crumbling straw, and he slid it into the spinning wheel's groove. A thin gold thread wound about the bobbin. Eliana gasped.

The faerie grinned. "Amazed?"

"Yes," she breathed, watching dumbfounded. She was an unpracticed spinner herself, and she had never seen a wheel used in the manner in which the faerie man used his. "I hardly believed it this morning, but to see you do it . . . You're wonderful!" Though she hardly knew why, tears pricked in her eyes once more.

"Why, thank you, Eliana," he replied. He continued to feed straw into the wheel, eyes fixed on his work. "I can do a few good things. Spin straw into gold, weave wool into silver, blow water into glass . . ." His voice trailed off as he looked up and put out a quick finger to catch the tear trailing down her cheek. The tear immediately solidified, turning into a drop of pure, crystalline glass on his fingertip. Eliana saw this and laughed, the rest of her tears immediately vanishing in delight.

The green-eyed man smiled charmingly and pocketed the glass teardrop before continuing his work.

"How did you know my name was Eliana?" she asked suddenly.

He looked up at her with some surprise. "Your name? Oh, well, I . . . lucky guess," he said, blushing. "It is a beautiful name."

She narrowed her eyes at him even as she continued to hand him straw. But then, he was a faerie. Was it really so strange that he should be able to guess her name? She decided not and decided as well to trust him. After some silence filled only with the sound of the treadle and the wheel, she said, "I think it only fair that you tell me your name in return."

He did not look up from his work but rather concentrated still more intently upon the tension of his whirling golden thread. "I do not have a name," he said at last with some reluctance. With a mirthless laugh, he added, "I'm afraid my parents forgot to name me when I was born."

Eliana frowned. "You cannot be serious."

"I am quite serious," he said, speaking through a forced smile. "I do not have a name."

She looked sadly at his skillful hands quickly twisting the straw fibers into a strand to be spun into delicate gold. "That's a shame," she whispered. "Everyone should have name."

The whirr of the spinning wheel filled the silence. After a thoughtful pause, Eliana said, "If it's any consolation, I don't think I have a home anymore. We're both missing something important."

He smiled. "So we are."

They worked on through the night until Eliana began to grow weary. Eventually her yawns made her more of a hindrance than a help. The faerie paused in his work to give her a gentle push toward the bed.

"Go lie down, lass," he said. "You have done enough for one night, and I will finish all this with time to spare."

She could not find the will to protest, but stumbled over to the bed and nestled into the pillow and blankets. As she closed her eyes, the sound of his voice reached out to her, gentle and sweet as a lullaby:

> *"Round about, round about,*
> *Lo and behold!*
> *Reel away, reel away,*
> *Straw into gold!"*

CHAPTER

10

Abandoned

Just at the brink of dawn, before the pink of the rising sun edged the rim of the sky, the green-eyed man rose from the spinning stool, stretched his back, and looked around at his handiwork, satisfied. He had done well, if he did say it himself. The piles of spun gold gleamed with their own otherworldly light, the richest, purest gold ever seen in all of this kingdom. If Hendry wasn't contented by this wealth, well . . .

Satisfaction faded from the faerie's eye as he turned his gaze from the golden bundles to the girl lying deeply asleep on her humble bed. Her dark hair fanned about her face, messy and yet somehow beautiful. She should be safe now. He had fulfilled his vow.

But this thought darkened the faerie's brow, and his heart moved with some emotion he feared to name.

He stepped lightly over to the bed, looking down into Eliana's peaceful face. Should he wake her to bid her farewell? King Oberon had forbidden him to return to her again, so this must be their final meeting. Surely it could not hurt to speak her name softly, to see those gentle eyes of hers flutter open and gaze at him one last time . . .

Somehow he knew that if she did wake, if she did look at him, he would never find the will to leave.

So he put out a hand, light as the gentlest breeze, and gently touched her soft cheek. "Good bye, Eliana," he whispered, lingering as long as he dared.

The next moment he was gone.

When the king and queen entered her gold-filled chamber, Eliana was awake and prepared. She stood quietly by the wall even as the door burst open and the queen rushed in, exclaiming loudly and plunging her hands deep into the largest of the gold piles. Eliana bobbed a curtsy to the king, but he did not seem to notice, standing thunderstruck in the doorway.

"You did it again!" he breathed at last. "You really, truly did it!"

No answer seemed to be required, so Eliana offered neither confirmation nor contradiction. She merely bobbed a second curtsy and stood with her hands folded. Her quiet demeanor belied the pounding of her heart, however. Would the king be satisfied with this abundance and let her go at last? Would she be permitted to return home . . . if she could even call it home after her stepmother's dreadful betrayal?

These thoughts crowded painfully behind Eliana's eyes. She could hardly say, even to herself, what she wanted in that moment. Freedom, certainly. But freedom to return to that life she had always known hardly seemed like freedom at all. Though she had managed to be content enough with her difficult lot these last two years, she found resistance forming in her heart now. Resistance and . . . and . . . what was this new emotion?

Why could she not, even now, standing in the intimidating presence of her king, get the memory of brilliant green eyes out of her head?

King Hendry, recovering himself at last, turned upon Eliana, his mustache lifting in an enormous grin. "You are a wonder! A shining gem!" he declared. "I did not believe you, but you really weren't lying."

Eliana said nothing. She merely bowed her head, dropping her gaze to the floor.

The king did not notice but continued in the same enthusiastic voice. "I'll make you a deal, girl: If you can do it just *one more time*, I'll name you a Lady of the Realm. How does that strike your ear?"

Ice froze Eliana's veins. Again? He wanted her to do the impossible . . . *again?* She couldn't speak, could hardly breathe! She could not even find the will to back away when the king approached her and took her cold hand in both of his warm ones.

"Spin the gold one more time," King Hendry continued, "and we shall have a dress made for you from the thread. You will be a shining image, and you will attend the Spring Advent Ball along with all the other eligible ladies of four kingdoms! Then we'll see what my son thinks of you," he added with another vast smile.

They moved her to another room, larger and richer than the cell she'd been kept in the past two days. A bed stood against the wall with pearly comforters and a draped canopy of pale voile, and the furnishings were made from mahogany. She walked on rugs of rich, woven threads softer than grass.

A maid came in, brushed Eliana's hair out and tied it up with delicate braids, dressed her, and gave her a basin of cool water. Eliana washed her face, put on her new dress the queen's seamstresses had made for her, and moved to the big curtain-hung windows. There she looked out upon the bright, beautiful day.

And saw the gallows still standing in the courtyard below.

Like one in a dream, she staggered to the bed and sank down on the edge of it.

"Will there be anything else, miss?" asked the maid, standing at the door.

Eliana blinked at her, hardly believing that such a phrase had been directed her way. She had never been waited on by anyone before in her life! "Oh, no. Not at all," she stammered.

"Very well, miss," said the maid, then curtsied prettily and exited the room.

Eliana sat like a statue in the stillness, hardly able to think, completely unable to move. A knock came at the door what seemed like hours later. She lacked the strength to speak, but they entered without her bidding, three servants carrying the spinning wheel, which they set in the center of the room.

The soldierly housekeeper came in as well. "I'm here to inform you of the doings of the past few days," she said, standing upright between Eliana and the spinning wheel. "Your mother, one Mistress Carlyn, has come inquiring about your welfare. She was sent away with assurances of your safety and given an invitation to the Spring Advent Ball to be held next week."

Eliana gaped. "The ball?" she whispered.

"Yes. Hosted in the prince's honor in hopes he will find a bride. Surely you've heard of it?"

She had, of course. Everyone knew about the Spring Advent Ball, three days of spectacular wonder, sumptuous and decadent. And everyone knew the particular significance of this year's event as well. Eliana nodded mutely.

"Our Sovereign Majesty wishes to introduce you at court on the third night of the ball at the Reveal. It is a masquerade, you understand, and everyone must wear a mask until the Reveal."

Eliana could think of nothing to say to this. But the housekeeper seemed to expect something, so she opened her mouth and asked bluntly, "Why must I spin more gold?"

"Because your king requests it."

"No," Eliana said, and her voice grew hard. "It's because the threat remains that I will be killed if I do not."

To this the housekeeper could give no answer.

"Why does the king *want* the gold?" Eliana persisted.

The housekeeper drew a long breath. Then she moved to the door and briefly paused on the threshold before turning back to say, "King Hendry will visit you tomorrow. It's best not to disappoint him."

With that, she left. Soon afterward, servant boys entered, carrying bale after bale of straw on their backs, then spools to hold the gold thread—dozens of them. Then the boys hastened out, and Eliana was alone once more. Alone with the spinning wheel and the straw.

Night fell.

Eliana waited . . .

. . . and waited . . .

. . . and waited.

When midnight came and the faerie did not appear, Eliana went to the bedroom door and tried to open it. It was locked. The clatter of guards could be heard outside, and she knew there would be no escaping that way. The window was high above the ground, and when she looked out she spied no ledges or vines she might use to climb down.

Seeing no other recourse, Eliana sat tentatively at the spinning stool. Trying her best to remember what the faerie man had done, she picked up handfuls of straw and ran them through the wheel. They crumbled to pieces and fell at her feet. She tried to be more careful, to spin more slowly. Then she tried spinning faster. But no matter what she did, she could not twist the dry grasses into thread.

Still the faerie did not come.

CHAPTER

II

The Power of a Name

The green-eyed faerie stared into the crystal ball, his hands grasping its smooth curves, his face pressed so near that his breath fogged the surface. His heart pounded with horror at what he saw.

Hendry wanted *more?*

The urge to fly back to the mortal world filled him with such power, he was almost away before reason caught up with him. But then came the memory — King Oberon's command.

"You may have one night, and no more!"

Loyalty to his master beat true in the faerie captain's breast. But that loyalty fell in direct conflict with other, equally powerful emotions. He gazed upon the image of Eliana waiting there in her lavish prison. Waiting for him, trusting in him, *needing* him . . .

His fingers let go of the crystal ball and moved almost unconsciously into the front of his tunic. They found the gold necklace and the ring secreted away there. Such lovely gifts, given without question despite the pain the giving caused. Truly he had never met a sweeter, more generous soul than that which was housed in this mortal girl's frame!

And must he leave her to suffer the fate intended for her by a greedy king?

"It seems to me singularly un-heroic for an ardent man to dither in the face of his lady's distress."

The nameless faerie turned guiltily at the sound of Queen Titania's voice. The beautiful queen glided beneath the tall pillars and took up a place on the far side of the crystal, her luminous eyes gazing upon the visions presented there. "The poor wee creature," she said, though there was a smile in her words. "Little does she know that her champion has grown faint-hearted at the last!"

"What would you have me do?" the faerie captain demanded, his voice sharp and choked. He knew he should never address his queen in such a manner, but distress made a fool of his civility. "How can I possibly disobey my king?"

Titania gave him a slow, sly look. Then she produced from under her long, sweeping robes a folded black garment. With a flick of her wrist she shook it out, and the faerie captain beheld a cloak of absolute darkness, deeper than night itself.

"If you would return to the mortal world without my husband noticing," said the queen, "there are ways this might be arranged."

The faerie captain stared at the cloak. Hope rose in his heart, momentarily drowning out his loyalty to Oberon.

"It is, after all, most unfair that the girl should die because my lordly husband is in a snit," Titania continued. "He can be most unreasonable at times, as we both well know." She handed the cloak to the captain, who accepted it without a word. "Go on, good man. Go rescue your lovely lass. Fulfill your vow to the fullest."

A number of protests rose up in the green-eyed man's throat. But his need to hasten to Eliana's side drove them all back down again. Without even daring to breathe a word of thanks, he donned the cloak, vanishing at once so completely that even Titania's quick eyes could not follow him. The next moment he sped away from this world to the other.

Titania chuckled softly to herself, shaking her head. Somehow she knew that her fun was just beginning!

With this thought in mind she turned from the crystal ball . . . in time to see King Oberon fill the open doorway across the room. She jumped in surprise then greeted him with an enormous, glorious smile. "Good evening, beloved husband!" she cried.

Oberon grunted and strode into the room. "Don't you try to distract me with your pretty face and pretty words, woman!" he said. "My good servant Puck tells me that he saw you making away with my cloak of darkness. And I want to know *why*."

"Since you don't need me anymore, I suppose I'll go back where I came from."

Eliana leapt up from the spinning stool, dropping the handful of straw she'd been futilely trying to twist into thread. Her shoulder bumped into the faerie man in her haste to turn around and face him. With a glad cry she flung her arms around his slender waist.

"What took you so long?" she exclaimed, her face buried in his chest. "I thought you'd gone for good!"

The faerie man drew a sharp breath then patted her head awkwardly. "I was unavoidably detained, dear one," he said gently. "But I'm here now. I'm here."

"I cannot do it on my own," Eliana said, pulling back, suddenly embarrassed. She put a hand to her flaming face, wishing she could hide her blushes from his quick gaze. "I tried, but . . ."

"I saw," said he, smiling down at her. "It was an abysmal effort at best! Apparently you did not inherit your mother's abilities."

Eliana frowned, shaking her head quickly. "I know it was a foolish effort, but I didn't know what else to try, and you didn't come and didn't come—"

He laughed then. "You make it sound as if I'd abandoned you!" When the girl was silent, he pulled her close and tucked her head under his chin. "I would never do such a thing."

Eliana shuddered and then relaxed into his embrace. As though confessing some guilty secret, she said, "King Hendry told me that I am to be presented to

his son at the Spring Advent Ball. I think he means for
. . . for us to marry."

The faerie startled at this, his face darkening even
as he held Eliana close. "So soon? Even though you've
never met?"

Her arms tightened about him, thrilling him to the
heart. "He'll still kill me, won't he? If I . . . if *you* don't
spin the gold?"

A long pause. Then the faerie man said, "I am not
sure. But I wouldn't put it past him."

At that, Eliana let go of the faerie and turned to the
spinning wheel dusted with crumbled bits of straw. She
could not bear to look at the faerie but hugged herself,
clutching her own arms with trembling fingers. "I have
nothing left to give you. The necklace and the ring were
all I had of any value."

"Is that true?" The faerie man moved soft-footed
around to the other side of the spinning wheel. His
brilliant eyes sought hers in the gloom, and she could
not help but meet his gaze. "Have you nothing else of
rare value that you might offer me? Willingly?"

Eliana stared deep into those eyes, seeing there a
longing she hardly dared name. A longing that
reflected her own? Could it possibly be that in those

eyes she saw the home she had lacked all these years? Could it possibly be that in her eyes he saw the same?

She spoke before realizing she intended to. "I will give you a name," she said. "Before dawn. I promise, I will name you."

His face lit up with an internal glow much brighter than all the gold he could ever spin. "Do you . . . do you realize what that means?" he asked her, his voice tight with hope and no little fear. "For faeries?"

As he spoke, realization struck Eliana. Deep inside, she knew then what she had promised — to name him was to claim him as her own. Forever. Such was the way of the Faerie Realm, the magic and beauty.

"Eliana," said he, "are you sure?"

She did not hesitate, not even for a moment. Even as another hot flush flamed in her cheeks, she smiled across the spinning wheel at him. "Yes," she said with absolute confidence. "I am sure."

For a moment she thought he would spring over the wheel and catch her in his arms. She rather hoped he would! But instead, with that brilliant light still shining like the sun in his face, out from his inmost being, he took a seat at the spinning stool. "Then let us get to work, my dearest one!" he cried. "In exchange for such a gift, I can spin whole mountains of gold!"

This time Eliana stayed up with him through the night. She handed him handful after handful of straw and dragged spools of thread away to another corner when they were full. The faerie sang loudly as he worked, and Eliana joined in the song, tentatively at first, and then with more vim:

> *"Round about, round about,*
> *Lo and behold!*
> *Reel away, reel away,*
> *Straw into gold!"*

Eliana stood close to the faerie now, kneeling beside the minuscule mound of straw left. She handed him a small handful, and he fed it in slowly. All the while, her mind busied itself with thinking of his name. It had to be the *right* name, the name that would truly claim him. Not just anything would do. Somehow it had to be a name that expressed all he had come to mean to her in so short a time, a name that expressed all he would come to mean to her as time went on.

"That's done!" the faerie declared at last. The sky outside the window was just beginning to lighten as he turned to Eliana and took her hands in his. Mounds of gleaming gold surrounded them both, but she could hardly see this for the bright glow of his eyes. "Now, my sweetest Eliana, may I claim that gift you promised?"

She smiled up at him, so full of joy in that moment. The name came to her then, the perfect name. *His* name. "Yes," she declared. "From this day forward, you will be called —"

A noise like a thunderclap filled the room, drowning out her voice. The sound itself was so powerful, it knocked Eliana to the ground. She thought she heard her faerie captain cry out in horror, but even that sound was lost in a powerful whirlwind that sent the gold thread flying from its neat piles and spools in a terrible maelstrom of light and darkness.

Suddenly Eliana's eyes fixed upon two sandal-clad feet. She looked up slowly into the most beautiful, most frightening face she could ever have imagined. Fear struck her mute, and she could not find the will even to scream.

King Oberon stared down at her. "What," he demanded, in a mountainous voice, "is the meaning of this?"

He lifted his gaze from her to the faerie, who had been blown across the room in the whirlwind, striking the wall hard. He picked himself up bravely, throwing back his shoulders as he faced his king.

"Master!" he cried, extending both hands. "Allow me to explain—"

"Don't bother!" Oberon roared. He flung out an arm, and suddenly enormous chains fastened themselves around his captain's wrists and neck, so heavy that they brought him crashing to his knees. "Titania has told me all, how you took my cloak of darkness and sneaked back into this world against my will. Did you really think you could get away with it? Did you really think me such a fool that I would not find out?"

"Please, my king!" the faerie cried, his horrified gaze moving from Oberon's terrible visage to the pale face of Eliana, who still lay upon the floor.

Oberon saw where his captain's gaze went, and he looked back down at Eliana. "What did you promise to give him in exchange for this magic of his?" he demanded.

Eliana tried several times to speak before finding her voice. "I—I promised to name him," she managed at last.

Lightning flashed in the faerie king's eyes. For he knew exactly what such a promise meant. His mouth warping into an angry snarl, he reached out and caught Eliana's head in a viselike grasp. He dragged her up to her knees, pulling her face close to his own so that she must stare deep into his eyes.

"You will forget," he said, enchantment lacing every word. "You will forget everything you have seen these last three nights. You will forget my captain, his face, his voice, his every word. I hereby strip you of all memory of him."

"*No!*" cried the captain, struggling against the heavy chains. "My king, I beg of you!"

But Oberon let go of Eliana, and she sank senseless to the floor, her dark hair spread out upon the rich carpet beneath her. The faerie king turned then to his captain and picked him up by his collar as though he weighed no more than a mewling kitten. "I'll teach you to compromise your loyalty to me!" he said.

Another wind whirled about the room, tossing the gold threads into tangles and snarls. But when it settled, each skein lay rolled as neatly as it had been before Oberon's arrival. In the center of the room stood the spinning wheel, and Eliana lay beneath it, pale as a ghost.

CHAPTER
12

Broken Hearts

A key slid into the bedroom door, and King Hendry entered a breath later with his queen two steps behind. Both stood in mute amazement, staring round at the piles and spools of shining gold, more gold than either had ever dared dream of in all their years as ruling monarchs.

Then King Hendry's eye lit upon the maid lying upon the floor. "Gracious me!" he exclaimed. "Is she dead?"

The next moment both king and queen, their servants crowding in behind them, knelt over Eliana. The queen felt for a pulse and breathed a grateful prayer when she found one—not out of any real concern for Eliana but rather from relief that they had not lost their gold-spinner.

"The labor may have been too taxing," King Hendry mused, sitting back on his heels and looking round at the mounds of gold. "She's not used to producing this much at a time, and we've worked her hard three nights running."

The queen stood and beckoned to her servants. "Take the gold to the royal treasury at once. And see that my ladies weave gold cloth for the finest dress! Lady Gold-Spinner must be presented on the third night of the Spring Advent Ball wearing a gown of her own creation."

The servants hastened to obey. As an afterthought the queen commanded them to lift Eliana up from the floor and place her gently on her bed as well. After all, it wouldn't do for a new lady of the realm to spend her day sleeping on the rug!

By the time Eliana stirred, the room was empty of the gold. King Hendry and his queen had slipped away long before, and only one serving maid sat perched on a low chair near Eliana's bed, ready to wait upon her new mistress the moment she awoke.

Eliana sat up, blinking in confusion. Her mind crashed with such a bewilderment of thoughts, she could not even hear the maid's queries after her health. She drew her knees up and pressed her aching forehead into them, willing the pounding in her head to subside.

At last some memories fell into order. She recalled coming to Craigbarr in the cart. She recalled the king's command to spin straw into gold. And . . . somehow, she had done it? How?

Her mother's necklace. And the ring. Both were gone. And her mother . . . yes, Mother had been a faerie! Somehow she knew that, though she could not remember how she knew. Was it her mother's magic that had enabled her to do the impossible? Lingering enchantment in the necklace and ring, used up to accomplish this strange request of the king's?

Something was missing. Something that hurt. The more she pressed into that emptiness where some important memory should be, the more the ache in her temples flared until she almost could not bear to think for pain.

"My lady!" exclaimed the maid. "Please, please, lie back. They say the magic has used you up, leaving you weak. You must rest and recover or you'll not be fit to attend the Spring Advent Ball next week!"

Eliana lifted her head and blinked blearily at the maid, a sweet-looking girl with buttercup-colored curls peeking out from under her maid's cap. Her kind, round eyes were full of concern, and Eliana allowed her fearful heart to trust in that homespun voice and obey its pleadings. She lay back on her pillow and let the maid soothe her head with cool cloths. Slowly the pain subsided.

"There, there," said the maid. "You'll soon be right as rain, my lady."

"Why do you call me that?" Eliana whispered. "Why do you call me 'my lady'?"

The maid blinked at her then smiled. "Because that's what you are! Or soon will be. King Hendry has declared that you will be named Lady Gold-Spinner on the third night of the Spring Advent Ball. You're to be given a fine estate in the country, lands to call your own, a stable of fine horses, and a houseful of servants! All in thanks for the great service you have rendered your sovereign." The maid's smile brightened still more, and her eyes gleamed with delight. "They say that the king and queen hope to see you wed Prince Ellis. Just so long as you take a liking to one another, of course."

Eliana closed her eyes. It was all too much, too much to consider! And why did the idea of marrying a prince fill her with so much . . . sorrow?

In the darkest, deepest chambers of the faerie king's palace, far from all sunlight, from all song, from all joy, the green-eyed man lay bent under the weight of his chains.

He wept softly in the darkness. Tears worth more than jewels trailed down his cheeks. Realizing this, he put a hand into his tunic front and withdrew his handkerchief—the same handkerchief that still held Eliana's precious tears. He caught his own tears now, letting them mingle with hers. At least in their sorrows they might be united. Even though they should never meet again.

How long would Oberon keep him bound in this dungeon? One century? Two? It hardly mattered to an immortal life. But the green-eyed man did not doubt that by the time he was released, Eliana would be dead and gone. Cherished in his memory, but lost to him forever.

At this thought he wept still more. In all his beautiful fey life he had never cried so much except for this girl. First, when she lost her father and he witnessed her so heartbroken. Now this, when he himself lay heartbroken . . .

And she? She would never think of him again. Not even as she might think of the memory of a dream.

A door opened somewhere in the darkness. Footsteps, feather-light like a dancer's tread, descended a long stair. The faerie captain looked up and saw luminous golden hair and two brilliant eyes like stars in the night.

Queen Titania stood over him, her arms folded, and shook her head. "Is this all that heroes are these days? Do they so easily break at the first breath of trouble?"

The green-eyed faerie drew himself up as straight as he could under those heavy chains. "I have crossed my king," he said, swallowing back his tears. Now shame rose in his heart, for he was a loyal soldier. "I have disobeyed him and now must suffer his wrath."

"Piffle!" said she with a toss of her head. "Had you not disobeyed, the girl would even now swing from the gallows! My husband takes whims into his head, unfair though they may be, and expects everyone to bow to his tyrannical will. It's not good for a man to be so absolutely obeyed in all things!"

The green-eyed man bowed his head and said nothing. The truth was, though he hated to flout the wishes of his master, he would do it all over again if it meant the difference between life and death for Eliana. He would lie here in the darkness of King Oberon's dungeons for a thousand years if it meant she might live a rich, full life, even without a single memory of him in her head. Perhaps she would marry the prince. Perhaps she would fall in love and live happily ever after.

Titania seemed to read these thoughts in his head. "What is this? Are you truly going to lie there like a limp rag? Get up, my man! Take action! You'll win your sweetheart yet!"

The green-eyed man stared up at his queen, unable to comprehend what she said. At last he said, "What would you have me do?"

She smiled. It was the most dangerous smile ever seen in all the worlds, and it was utterly beautiful. "Make something for me. Use your secret powers and make what I ask. If you will do this, I promise you, everything will turn out right in the end."

"Make what, my queen?" he asked.

She whispered the answer in his ear.

CHAPTER
13

Feigned Pleasantries

"*Mistress Carlyn and Misses Bridin and Innis, my lady.*"

Eliana sat in the window, gazing out across the courtyard and the city into the countryside beyond, like a prisoner gazing out to freedom. She turned at the sound of her maid Martha's voice and saw the sweet girl bobbing a curtsy in the doorway.

The next moment her stepmother and two stepsisters, clothed in their shabby finery, swept into the room.

"*Dearest* Eliana!" exclaimed Mistress Carlyn, and flew across the room, catching Eliana in an embrace before the girl had a chance to dodge her clutching hands. "Bridin, Innis, and I have been *so worried* for you! Of course we knew, we just *knew* that somehow you would prove your worth to the king and queen, but *still . . .*"

Eliana pulled back sharply, standing up from the window seat and putting some distance between herself and her stepmother. Her clothing, though the simplest she'd been able to find, was finer by far than anything Mistress Carlyn wore, and she saw how her stepmother looked her up and down with envy in her cold eyes and jealousy behind her insincere smile.

This woman had tried to have her killed. Inadvertently, perhaps, but the fact remained. And now she dared to call her 'dearest' and to claim concern? It made Eliana's stomach turn.

She moved away from Mistress Carlyn and addressed herself to her stepsisters instead. "Bridin. Innis. How are you both?"

They both offered awkward curtsies, and Innis managed a small smile. "We're well, Eliana," she murmured.

"And how is Grahame? And all the animals?"

"They're well too," Innis said. "Grahame sends his

best—"

"Oh, *don't* bother your sister with all of that!" Mistress Carlyn cried, seating herself as grandly as she could in the finest chair in the chamber. "Did you hear, Eliana? Your sisters and I have been invited to attend the Spring Advent Ball along with you tomorrow night. Is that not most grand and glorious?"

Eliana could think of nothing to say in response to this. For the last week she had dreaded the coming ball. Now she might have to attend it in company with this false family of hers? She could only hope that the crowds would be so dense that she might effectively avoid them through the three nights of festivity.

"Tell me, Eliana, do tell me," Mistress Carlyn persisted, leaning forward in her seat, her eyes full of eager ambition. "They say that you are to be betrothed to the prince on the third night of the ball. Is this true?"

Eliana's mouth went dry. "I don't know," she said simply and honestly.

"Because just *think* what it would mean for your family!" Mistress Carlyn persisted. "Why, dukes and lords would come courting your sisters, given the opportunity to marry into the royal family itself! Surely you must think of their futures, dear girl. After all, we have looked after you throughout these last two years . . ."

Eliana glanced at Bridin and Innis, who at least had the good grace to look ashamed. They stared at their folded hands, still standing close to the door as though they would make a quick escape if given half a chance. Not for the first time, Eliana pitied them. It could not be easy to live under the thumb of such a mother.

"Well, tut," said Mistress Carlyn, when no answers to her questions were forthcoming. "If you don't know, you don't know. But surely you must know when you will take possession of your new estate? I understand it is very grand indeed, with rolling farm fields and a lake and woodlands. You'll no doubt remain on at court after the betrothal, but I thought your sisters and I might move in as soon as possible. We've already put the mill up for sale, of course, and . . ."

She prattled on, and Eliana ceased listening. She could not believe anything that was said, could not believe that this had become her life. How in heaven's name had she come from her father's humble mill to be here in the king's palace, listening to Mistress Carlyn discuss the bountiful wealth that was soon to be hers?

How had she managed to do the impossible? To spin straw into gold?

The question burned across her mind, and Eliana frowned at the return of the sudden searing headache. With a little moan she sat down on a low seat, putting her head in her hand.

Maid Martha, observing all, quickly stepped into action. "My lady is fatigued," she declared in a forceful voice. "She is still recovering from her exertions of a week ago. You must all leave now and give her time to rest so that she may be fresh and ready for tomorrow night's ball."

With this cheerful urging she managed to get Mistress Carlyn up from her seat and out the door, Bridin and Innis hastening on her heels. She shut the door in their wake and turned back to Eliana, hastening to her side. "Dear lady!" she said, taking Eliana by the hand. "Let's get you back to bed."

Eliana allowed herself to be helped up and to her bed. A week had not yet accustomed her to being served by another, but Martha had such a homey way about her, and her sweetness was hard to resist.

"You'll forgive my saying so," Martha murmured as she fetched a cool basin of water and applied a damp cloth to Eliana's pounding forehead, "but that Mistress Carlyn . . . she don't seem much like you. I would never have guessed she was your mother!"

"Stepmother," Eliana whispered. "My mother died years ago."

"Oh, I am right sorry to hear that," said Martha. "Now she, I am sure, was a fine and beautiful lady worthy of crowns and diadems! A real princess."

"She was," Eliana replied, closing her eyes. "She was indeed."

A tear slipped down her cheek and dampened her pillow. But the headache did at last subside.

CHAPTER
14

Mischief Making

Queen Titania stood in the pillared room, gazing into the crystal upon the mortal world. She saw the preparations at Craigbarr, making ready for the grand ball. Or grand by human standards . . . compared to the nightly festivities of King Oberon's court, this mortal ball was like a simple peasant dance!

Her curious eye sought out the girl, the mortal miss who had so entranced the green-eyed faerie. She saw her pacing her rooms, a ball gown spread out upon her bed. Soon they would dress her up like a little doll and send her out among all the great lords and ladies of four kingdoms. Poor child! She was not meant for a life like this.

Titania watched all, various plans forming in her mind. Then with a sudden sweep of her long sleeves, she whirled about and descended the tower stair. Down, down, down she went, plunging into a still deeper stairwell leading far underground, far from all sunlight and song. She came at last to the dungeon chamber where the green-eyed man even now worked at the project she had assigned to him.

She peered between the bars of the chamber door. There he sat cross-legged, his hands hard at work, his cheeks puffed up with careful blowing. He wasn't finished yet, but he was close. Very close indeed.

She opened the door as though the locks and bolts meant nothing — for indeed they could mean nothing to her, queen of all this realm. The green-eyed man looked up from his labors and carefully set aside the work of his hands. He rose, struggling against his chains, and offered a stiff bow.

"Leave off your work for now, good captain," said Titania with an imperious smile. "I have a much jollier task for you tonight!"

"And what might that be, Your Majesty?" he asked with grave politeness.

Titania smiled.

"Oh, my lady!" Martha clasped her hands beneath her chin, her eyes shining. "You look positively *beautiful!*"

The team of ladies-in-waiting who worked on Eliana gave Martha sharp glares, for a mere maid should not speak in the presence of her mistress unless spoken to first. But in the last week Eliana had struck up a friendship with Martha, with whom she had much more in common than anyone else in the palace, and Martha too easily forgot her place.

Eliana, standing in the center of those fancy ladies with their fancy airs and fancy clothes, looked over their heads to meet her maid's eye. The admiration she saw there did not give her much comfort. If anything, she felt even more nervous than she had before!

The golden gown being specially made for her was not yet ready. The seamstresses worked on it night and day, intending to have it complete for the third night of the ball. But on this, the first night, Eliana was clad in deep blue, the neck and sleeves edged in little winking crystals like stars shimmering in reflection on a lake's rippling surface. Her long hair had been brushed and brushed until it shone, then held away from her face with a simple silver band. Eliana was relieved that she wasn't shoved into layers of silk and veils and feathers, but even so, the richness of the cloth unnerved her, and the silver headpiece felt too much like a crown for comfort.

She could not bring herself to look in the mirror when it was brought to her, but dropped her eyes and stared at the floor instead.

"And here is your mask, Lady Gold-Spinner," one of the ladies said, presenting Eliana with a lovely mask shaped like a crescent moon surrounded by the golden rays of the sun. When she put it on, it covered all but the corners of her mouth.

Now she felt she could dare looking into the mirror, for she was so well disguised that she did not even recognize herself. The moon-and-sun mask complimented the starry gown beautifully. She could not help a little gasp of surprised delight.

"The time has come," said a voice in the doorway. Eliana turned and saw the housekeeper herself standing there, looking more regal in her uniform than any of the ladies-in-waiting in their finery and flounces. "Your escort is here, Lady Gold-Spinner."

Eliana peered beyond the housekeeper and saw four men-at-arms standing in the passage. What, was she to be escorted about the place like a prisoner even now, on the night of the ball? Did they think she would try to flee, attempt to slip away unnoticed in such a gown?

She said nothing however. What could be the good of protesting? Instead, she gathered up her heavy skirts and passed to the door. She paused on her way to momentarily clasp Martha's hand for a bit of friendly support. Martha gave her an encouraging smile. "Have a wonderful time, lady!" she said.

Eliana made no answer but passed through the door and into the company of the men-at-arms. Flanked on either side, she allowed herself to be led through the splendid galleries of Craigbarr, down to the glorious ballroom.

Music reached up to greet her before all else, music more gorgeous than anything she had ever before heard. That, at least, would be a real pleasure of the evening—the opportunity to hear the kingdom's most talented musicians working their magic on various instruments.

The next moment, she came to the edge of the balcony overlooking the ballroom, and the sight struck her with such a wave of intimidation that she nearly lost the will to move! Such colors! Such movement! Such light! It was all too much, too overwhelming. The noblest lords and ladies of four kingdoms milled around below, some dancing, some talking, some partaking of delicacies from the refreshment tables. Eliana had thought her own garments rich, but now she felt poor and shabby indeed as she looked upon all the jewels and furs.

King Hendry and his queen stood partway up the stair, receiving visitors as they arrived. They wore coronets upon their heads and ermine-lined cloaks over their shoulders. Their masks were of a lion and a tiger, but they weren't large enough masks to effectively hide the identity of either monarch.

And just beyond them stood Prince Ellis. But Eliana couldn't get a good glimpse of him.

One of the men-at-arms coughed. Taking the hint, Eliana forced her limbs back into motion, allowing her escort to lead her down the stair. King Hendry turned at her approach, his mustache lifting with a smile of greeting. "Ah! Lady Gold-Spinner!"

The queen turned at her husband's voice, and both greeted Eliana warmly. Eliana curtsied the best she knew how, feeling what a poor offering it was. Miller's daughters were not trained in the social niceties of court, and she could tell by the way the queen blinked that she had not quite got it right.

King Hendry took her by the hand, however, and raised her to her feet. "Away with you," he told the men-at-arms, dismissing them. "And you, dear girl, must enjoy yourself tonight," he continued, patting Eliana's hand. "I hope you are well recovered from your labors?"

"Yes, Your Majesty," Elaina said softly. She decided not to mention the headaches which still plagued her every time she thought about those hazy three nights she'd spent with the spinning wheel.

"Good, good!" said Hendry, his smile widening. "Now continue on your way in, and be certain to make your best curtsy to Ellis as you go. He is *most* anxious to meet you and will, no doubt, beg you the honor of a dance."

Eliana felt as though her heart would burst from between her ribs. She curtsied again to both king and queen then, clutching her skirts so hard that her fingers hurt, continued down the steps.

A cluster of people surrounded Prince Ellis, who stood on the third step of the stairway, above the rest of the crowd but lower than his parents. Eliana could just catch a glimpse of a blue mask that seemed vaguely aquatic — a sea god, perhaps? The king had commanded her to make herself known to the prince, and she did not think she could disobey so easily. The small cluster of people, seeing her approach, whispered and made way so that a path cleared itself before her. There was nothing for it! She must meet the prince.

Eliana bravely lifted her chin and started forward . . . when suddenly she found herself standing no longer on the stair but on the other side of the ballroom. Open doors stood behind her; turning her head, she looked out into cool, lush gardens. Looking ahead at the crowded ballroom, she could just see the stairway where the royal family stood.

Had she curtsied to the prince? She couldn't quite remember but didn't think she had. Had she even seen him? How had she come to be here? She frowned behind her mask, feeling a little faint and very uncertain of herself.

She did not see the golden-haired woman who

laughed to herself and darted away among the ball guests, leaving behind no trace save for an exotic and intoxicating perfume.

Eliana decided not to try to make her way back to the stair. If Prince Ellis wished to seek her out he may, but she wasn't obligated to attract his attention. She moved quietly among the guests on the edge of the ballroom, avoiding their curious gazes whenever they turned her way. She looked for but did not see Mistress Carlyn or her two stepsisters, though she did not doubt they had turned up in their shabby best to rub elbows with the elite.

After no more than half an hour of quietly making herself seem smaller than she was, Eliana stood once more near the garden door, longing to slip out into the coolness of the night and wander among the blooming shrubs and trees. Movement caught her eye, and she turned to see a man at least a head taller than she was approach and bow to her. His mask shaped like several oak leaves was bronzed over.

"What is a lovely lady like you doing away from everyone else?" said he. "You should be socializing with all the young men. I hear that the prince himself is perusing the crowds tonight, seeking a proper bride."

He smiled at her.

For a moment she thought perhaps she recognized that smile. But the moment passed.

"I cannot find courage within myself," she admitted softly, ducking her head. "Since the crowds are so pressing, it did not seem worth it."

"I've just come from the depths of the throng myself," he said, "and I am sorry to confirm that what you say is true." He offered her something, and she realized that he had brought her a glass of sweet cider. She accepted it gratefully, and he, taking her smile as encouragement, leaned against a pillar next to her. "All of this shouting, beguiling, and dancing is enough to make one die from overstimulation."

Eliana chuckled at this exaggeration. "But you must be used to it by now," she said. "This is my very first ball."

The stranger bowed his head. "Then it is a pleasure to share the experience with you. May I ask your name, my lady?"

She wondered if she should call herself Lady Gold-Spinner, as the king and the ladies-in-waiting had referred to her. But she would not officially receive the title until the third night of the ball, so perhaps she need not claim it yet. "My name is Eliana," she said instead.

"That is a beautiful name."

The sensation of familiarity struck her again. With it came the very faintest edge of pain around her temples. She shook this away quickly, taking a sip of cool cider. But she could not stop herself from asking, "May I ask your name in return, good sir?"

The man did not answer right away, and the smile that slowly spread across his face was not altogether happy.

Just then, a group of dancing couples stumbled a bit too far from the dancing floor, nearly bumping into the pair. The man in the oak-leaf mask quickly jumped in front of Eliana, pushing back the giddy gentry when they pressed too close. Eliana blushed deeply behind her mask, looking down into her cider glass, afraid to look anywhere else lest her eyes betray her. The oak-leaf man turned to make certain she was all right.

"I'm fine," she answered quickly. "Just a bit startled."

Her question was forgotten in the tumult. The oak-leaf man began to entertain her by pointing out the people of particular note milling about amid the masses. The one in the wolf mask, he told her, governed the province of Flostrin, and the fair hawk beside him was his wife—a much younger woman than her lordly husband, though the way she patted his arm seemed fond enough. They were rumored to be quite a doting pair despite the age difference, the oak-leaf man confided to Eliana.

Now the portly man laughing robustly was the Duke of Dravint, his good humor unable to be disguised even by the ferocious boar mask he wore. And that woman wearing a fox mask? She was the lovely princess of Syntorell. Rumor had it she had come tonight hoping to snare Prince Ellis for herself.

On and on the list went, from the earl in the stag mask to the baronet wearing the face of a hare. And for each one the oak-leaf man related some sort of secret quirk or fact to interest and entertain Eliana.

The hours flew swiftly past. Everyone grew louder, attempting to make their voices heard, until the deafening roar throbbed in Eliana's ears. Nausea slithered in her stomach and slid up her throat. The air was thick with the stench of a hundred and more people gathered in too small a place, making it difficult for her to breathe.

The oak-leaf man touched her arm in concern. "Are

you feeling unwell?"

Eliana tried bravely to brush off the nausea and take a step. But the dizziness returned tenfold. She shook her head slowly. "I'm sorry. The heat . . ."

"Let us step outside into the garden then," said he. "Fresh air should set you right."

Once escaped from the thunderous sounds and the smells, Eliana could breathe and think again. She drew a deep breath and slumped down onto a bench beside a trellis of sweet peas. The pretty pink flowers looked red in the torchlight, and the man's mask took on a magical gleam. She could see his eyes sparkling through the eye holes.

"Thank you so much," she said, still sounding a little weak. "It was suffocating in there."

"It is my pleasure, dear lady. Considering this is your first ball, you have done quite well. I did not last so long my first time!"

"How long did you last?"

He laughed. "I ran off before the herald finished introducing me."

Eliana laughed as well, covering her mouth with her hand. It felt odd to have the mask on, but she dared not take it off. No one was supposed to remove their masks until the third night Reveal.

The man took a seat on the bench beside her and leaned his head far back, gazing up into the sky. "The stars are beautiful tonight," he whispered.

Eliana followed his upward gaze to see the clear dark blanket of night. Constellations shone brightly like falling snowflakes. "I've never seen the sky so clear before," she said. Where she had grown up, the forests were too thick for such an astral view.

"Now that is a shame," said her companion. He smiled at her suddenly and, standing, held out his hand. "I was wondering, if I might be so bold . . . Would you honor me with this dance, my lady?"

The music was still audible over the ruckus inside. The strings hummed and the horns sang low. It was a spritely air that sang to Eliana's very heart! Her feet could not resist, and she accepted his outstretched hand, allowing him to pull her lightly to her feet.

Few men had ever danced with her before. Her father did not count, since she'd been a little girl, hardly up to his waist, and he'd been teaching her. She still felt like a little girl, for her head scarcely reached this man's shoulder, and she tripped over his feet once or twice. But he did not correct her. He only smiled with great enthusiasm as if she were the greatest dancer in the world and it was a pleasure simply to be with her.

Eliana felt her heart stir with an emotion both familiar and unfamiliar all at once. What was this feeling? Was it love? Certainly not the deep love that couples often marry for; that sort of love takes a little more time. But it might be the kind of love someone feels when meeting with genuine kindness after months and years of receiving no affection at all.

The music slowed and faded from their hearing. The oak-leaf man smiled and bowed elegantly, sweeping his short cape like the wings of a pretty songbird. Eliana laughed and curtsied back, a more graceful curtsy than she'd ever before managed. Something about this man and his nearness gave her confidence and, in turn, grace.

"Thus concludes my time here with you, Lady Eliana," said her companion. "I'm afraid I must be going."

"Oh. You are leaving me?" Eliana wished she could somehow retrieve the words, embarrassed that she would speak so boldly.

But the oak-leaf man's eyes glinted behind his bronze mask. "I could never leave you," he said, his voice strangely deep and serious. "But I must depart for now. I promise to return tomorrow. And in the meanwhile . . ."

He took Eliana by the hand. The next instant, something cool slipped onto her finger.

"To remember me by," the oak-leaf man whispered.

Eliana blinked. In that brief lowering of her lashes, he vanished. Though she looked all around the garden for him, she saw not even the briefest glimpse of his fluttering cloak or a gleam of light shining off his mask. From somewhere distant she heard the toll of a distant church bell booming out the hour: twelve deep, rolling tones.

Eliana looked down at her hand. There on her finger gleamed a bright gold ring.

CHAPTER

15

Forgotten Memories

The stroke of twelve resounded in the mortal world, and the rolling vibrations rippled through time and space. A doorway opened between worlds, and the faerie captain, no longer clad in festival finery, stepped back into the darkness of his dungeon cell.

Queen Titania sat upon a lowly bench waiting for him. Her presence made that bench seem like a throne.

"Well, brave swain?" said she, smiling to see him appear. "You have fulfilled your part of this bargain and returned no later than midnight. But how were those intermittent hours whiled away? Satisfactorily, I trust?"

The nameless faerie took the oak-leaf mask from his face. The moment he did so, it fell into pieces, dried oak leaves drifting to the ground at his feet. His expression, now revealed, was not full of the happy smiles Titania had anticipated.

"I don't think it worked," he said sadly, forgetting to bow in the presence of his queen. He ran a hand through his hair and sighed. "I placed the ring upon her finger, and I hoped the power of her mother's gift would be enough to counter King Oberon's spell. But I don't believe she remembered me."

Titania's lovely face twisted in a momentary scowl. Then she shook this away with a smile more brilliant than usual. "Well, it was worth a try. And I have more tricks up my sleeve!"

So saying, she moved her trailing sleeve, revealing the shining object upon which the green-eyed faerie had been working the last several days of his imprisonment. "Coming along nicely, I should say," she purred, touching it lightly with one finger. "Will the other be ready by the time I stipulated?"

"I believe so, Your Majesty," the green-eyed faerie said. "As long as—"

He broke off when Titania sat suddenly upright,

one hand upraised. The next instant, his queen vanished, her body blending into the stones of the wall and the floor, her hair becoming nothing more than moss and lichen. She disappeared so completely that the green-eyed man almost forgot she had been sitting there at all. He opened his mouth, puzzled, uncertain what to say or do . . .

The dungeon door opened behind him. King Oberon's voice spoke: "Well, captain, have you learned your lesson?"

A thrill of terror electrified the captain so that he momentarily could neither speak or move. Then he whirled and bowed deeply to his king, who stood in the doorway, arms folded. "Your Majesty!" he exclaimed. "I—I—"

"Certainly is gloomy enough in here," said King Oberon, looking around the cell, his mouth curled with distaste. "How long have I had you holed up? I forget."

"Well," said the captain. He didn't want to say that the time had been nowhere near so long as he'd expected. Nor did he want to say that it was ages, for he hated to lie.

King Oberon did not seem to expect an answer. "I need you back on duty," he said. "No one keeps the men in line as well as you do, and I don't want to be caught short-handed should the goblins decide to pay us an unwelcome visit. So if you've quite learned to behave yourself, I'll let you out. Agreed?"

The nameless faerie bowed again, his deepest, most graceful bow. "I will endeavor in all things to conduct myself with honor and integrity," he said with deep sincerity.

Satisfied, Oberon beckoned him out. He did not seem to notice that his man no longer wore the heavy fetters with which he himself had bound him. His mind was occupied with the intrigues of the faerie court, both big and small, and he could not even fully recall why he had punished his captain in the first place.

So the two of them exited the dungeons and climbed the winding stairs. When they had gone, a certain patch of stones, shadows, and moss resolved back into the lovely face and form of Titania.

She laughed to herself with utmost delight. There was nothing in all the worlds she enjoyed more than thwarting her husband's tyrannical will! Indeed, she knew he would not love her half so well if she were not skilled at making his life difficult.

What a delicious game this had turned into!

"Oh, my lady! Did you have the most wonderful time?"

Eliana, relieved to find only Martha waiting for her when she at last returned to the quiet of her own rooms, sank into a chair and pulled the mask from her face. Seeing how flushed her lady was, Martha hastened to bring her a glass of water, which Eliana accepted gratefully.

"Was it more beautiful than beautiful?" Martha asked, eager for details. "I tried to sneak to the balcony rail and get a peek, but the housekeeper saw me and shooed me away. I heard the music though! And I glimpsed some of the fine ladies in their gowns. It must have been a garden of delights!"

No answer presented itself to Eliana. How could she explain the overwhelming crush of people? The heat? The fear?

And how could she explain the exquisite beauty of a kind man's voice? Of a gentle hand leading her out into the cool of the garden? How could she explain the loveliness of sweet-pea blossoms compared to the jewels of all the ladies of all the realms?

Martha, sensing her lady's exhaustion, prattled on sweetly without pressing for answers even as she helped Eliana out of her gown and brushed out her long hair, preparing her for bed. But she could not resist asking at one point, "Did my lady meet the prince?"

"Well . . . no," Eliana admitted. And this was strange, she considered in the privacy of her mind. After all, King Hendry required her presence only so that she would meet and marry his son. Yet somehow she had managed to pass the whole night without a single interaction with Prince Ellis.

"That is a shame," Martha said, putting back the covers of Eliana's bed and then tucking her lady in. "Prince Ellis is such a fine man. No doubt you will meet him tomorrow night and dance with him too."

While Martha bustled about, putting out candles and tidying up the discarded ballroom finery, Eliana lay quietly propped against her pillows. She studied the gold ring on her finger. A simple band with no adornment. It could be any ring, any ring at all.

So why did she know—know with absolute conviction—that it was her mother's own ring returned to her at last?

How had she lost it? Was it when her stepmother

threw it away in the ashes, declaring it nothing more than trash? Or was it during those three nights of spinning, which seemed weirdly hazy in her memory? One way or another, lose it she had, and her heart had ached at the loss.

But how in the world did the oak-leaf man get it? How did he know it would mean so much to her?

Memory plucked at her conscious mind. But with it came the searing pain that had become all too familiar during her stay at Craigbarr. Eliana could not help the moan that escaped her lips as she sank back into her pillows. The pain swept over her in a hideous wave.

"Oh no!" exclaimed Martha. "Is it that bad headache again?" She spent the next hour soothing Eliana's forehead with cool cloths until at last her lady fell into a deep but troubled sleep.

In her dreams Eliana heard the oak-leaf man saying, "*To remember me by . . . To remember me by . . .*"

CHAPTER
16

Of Dancing and Games

The following night the ladies-in-waiting returned to Eliana's room, this time bringing with them a gown of silver edged in blue stones. It was more elegant and lovely than her dress of the previous night, but Eliana knew it would pale in comparison to the gold dress which was even now being finished by the queen's team of industrious seamstresses.

She was relieved when the same mask was brought to her. She had worried that if her mask were changed, perhaps the oak-leaf man would not recognize her in the crowds. But then, would she recognize him? She had not, she realized long after the fact, succeeded in getting his name from him the night before.

"Tonight I'll ask again," she whispered even as the ladies styled her hair and placed jewels about her neck.

One lady lifted Eliana's hand, prepared to slide a ring into place. She paused, frowning, and said, "What is this?" indicating the gold band Eliana already wore.

"Oh. Please, I would much rather wear it," Eliana said, which wasn't really an answer, but she didn't know what else to say.

The lady looked at the ring again, comparing it to the small starburst of gems she held. "It's very plain, Lady Gold-Spinner," she said.

Eliana nodded, and her cheeks flushed a soft rose hue. "It was my mother's," she whispered.

The lady looked for a moment as though she might protest. But then something like understanding seemed to pass over her face. She shrugged and put away the starburst ring.

A knock at the door; Martha hurried to answer it. Once more, men-at-arms waited just outside, ready to escort Eliana to the ball.

"Your mask, Lady Gold-Spinner," said one of the ladies.

Eliana slid the moon-and-sun mask into place,

lifted the hem of her voluminous skirts, and stepped out among the guardsmen.

King Hendry and his queen stood again on the steps above the ballroom, greeting guests as they arrived. King Hendry pushed his lion mask up onto his forehead when he saw Eliana approach, fixing her with a terrible gaze that made her knees tremble. "I understand you did *not* dance with my son last night," he said, his voice a growl that matched his mask all too well.

Eliana tried to curtsy, teetering dangerously in her nervousness. "Forgive me, Your Majesty!" she said. "Your son did not ask me to dance."

"Didn't he?" Hendry shot a glare over his shoulder to where the prince stood, several steps further down, laughing with the fox-masked Princess of Syntorell. "Didn't he . . ."

The next moment Eliana found her elbow held in the king's tight grasp, and she nearly tripped as he dragged her down the stairs. "Ellis!" he bellowed.

So this was how she would meet the prince, the man she was expected to marry. Pushed at him against his will by his angry father. Eliana's face flamed so hot behind her mask that she feared it might melt down her cheeks. If only she could slip away! If only she could . . .

She blinked. Then she drew a deep, gasping breath.

For she found herself standing under the pillars near the garden door, far across the crowded ballroom from the king and his son. And, somehow, she still had not been introduced to Prince Ellis!

Though her beauty outshone that of every other woman in that room, no one saw the golden-haired lady who stood in the shadows by the grand staircase. She did not wish to be seen, so a veil of mystery covered her, shielding her from all eyes. Even those who half caught a glimpse — a glimpse of loveliness that would rival the most glorious spring sunrise — wandered away in a blinking daze, wondering why their hearts suddenly hurt with nameless longing.

Queen Titania listened to the angry voice of King Hendry just above her.

"I *told* you I wanted you to dance with her tonight! She's going to be your *bride*, and I need you to be *seen* with her at this ball *before* the Reveal!"

"I know, Father," Prince Ellis replied sullenly. "I

haven't seen her though. I mean I don't know what she looks like, if you'll remember, and she's wearing a mask anyway. If you happen to spot her, point her out to me, and I'll introduce myself."

"You'd better!" King Hendry raged, little caring if nearby guests heard him over the sweet strains of music playing. "You'd better dance with her till her feet bleed!"

"Whatever you say, Father," said the prince, heaving a deep sigh.

Titania chuckled merrily like a lightly babbling brook, sending ripples of mirth out from her shadowy hiding place and making all the mortals nearby smile, though they couldn't have said why. Then she looked out across the crowds, searching for the girl in her moon-and-sun mask and for that beautiful bronze mask of oak leaves she had carefully repaired for the faerie captain. Surely he had arrived by now. Where had the two of them gotten off to?

In her eagerness to spy the lovers, she completely missed the mischievous little imp face peering down at her from a high perch in the chandelier over her head.

"Oh, what a naughty majesty you are!" Oberon's servant Puck whispered, and giggled so hard that the chandelier shook and wax dripped from its candles to spatter on the floor far below.

Eliana waited near the pillars, hoping the oak-leaf man would search for her there. Time passed, and he did not come.

Masked strangers nodded to her, possibly recognizing her moon-and-sun mask from the night before, though they did not know the lady who hid behind it. She always smiled in response, a nervous smile, and hoped none of them would stop and try to speak to her. She did not know how to talk to these nobles and dignitaries, and the idea of trying to navigate the difficult waters of courtly conversation filled her with dread.

She looked down at the gold ring on her finger. What a comfort it was here among all this glittering glamour! So simple, so plain—so beautiful like her mother.

"*To remember me by,*" the oak-leaf man had said. Why would he say such a thing? It sounded as though he intended to leave her forever, with nothing more than a token by which to recall her one delightful evening in his presence. But had he not promised to return to her tonight?

"I hoped I would find you here."

The longed-for voice shot through her heart. Eliana looked up through the eyeholes of her mask, and there stood her oak-leaf man, his face lit up with a smile.

"May I have the honor of this dance?" he asked, much as he had the night before in the garden.

Eliana did not even speak an answer. She merely gave him her hand, and he swept her onto the dance floor, right out into the center. Her stomach turned with terror that was not altogether unpleasant to find herself so deep in the throng of merry-makers. But the oak-leaf man's hand guided her with gentle confidence, and she relaxed into his hold, trusting him completely. Her knowledge of the complicated steps was faulty at best, but with him as her partner, she did not think she disgraced herself too badly.

They danced through an entire set. Then the oak-leaf man raised a hand, signaling to the musicians. By some magic, they understood him and immediately started playing a new tune—a simple tune, one that Eliana knew quite well.

"The Cobbler's Reel!" she exclaimed, laughing up

into the oak-leaf man's smiling face. "This is just a village dance!"

"But much livelier than any of the tunes we've had yet, don't you agree?"

"Oh, absolutely!" Eliana lifted the hem of her skirt with one hand, her feet lightly picking out the spritely paces of this reel, which she knew very well indeed. Yes, it was merely a country dance, silly and ungainly compared to the stately tunes of court. But the grace of a spring breeze lifted her spirits, and she whirled with her partner, her skirts fluttering like the petals of a silver rose. Through it all he smiled, and his smile was so beaming that an intoxication like wine filled Eliana's head at the mere sight of it.

The song came to an end. The musicians blinked as though waking from a daze then started back to work, playing a much more somber melody. Eliana cast the oak-leaf man a regretful glance but then placed a hand to her racing heart. The Cobbler's Reel had left her winded.

He led her from the floor back to their quiet corner near the garden door. "One moment," he said, and slipped away, returning soon after with a cooling drink, which she accepted gratefully.

She noticed then the color of his eyes. The oak-leaf mask was so intricate, and his smile so bright, she had hardly bothered to look beyond them before. Now she saw that his eyes, peering at her through the eyeholes, were a color she had never before seen on a man — a bright green, like a blade of grass.

His smile softened, and something about his gaze held her transfixed. "Eliana," he said gently, "you really are beautiful."

She blushed and managed to tear her gaze away, looking down at her glass of cider instead. "How would you know? I'm wearing a mask."

He shook his head. "Beauty is not a matter of appearance. It's about what is inside you."

Suddenly his eyes locked onto the edge of the crowd. Without a word he caught Eliana by the elbow and whisked her away to the other side of the pillar.

"What's wrong?" she asked breathlessly.

"Nothing. Nothing at all." He hardly seemed aware of her just then, gazing around the pillar, his mouth a grim line. "There was just . . . someone I thought I recognized."

"It wasn't my stepmother, was it?" Eliana asked with a nervous laugh. Craning her neck, she barely made out the plume of a shabby mask across the room. Something about the angle of that head reminded her of Mistress Carlyn, and she wondered if her stepfamily had come to this night of the ball after all, though she had yet to meet them.

"I'm not the only one avoiding someone, I see," the oak-leaf man said, grinning down at her then.

She glanced up at him then frowned slightly. "Before I forget . . . What is your name, good sir?"

His grin froze, remaining on his face only by an effort. "Do you not know?"

"You never told me."

He bowed his head down close to her own. One of his large hands took one of hers, and his fingers pressed against her gold ring. "But perhaps . . . perhaps you remember?"

There it was—that memory, so close! So very close, she almost could lay hold of it!

But with it came the pain.

Eliana gasped, and if the oak-leaf man had not possessed such quick reflexes, her cider glass would have shattered on the floor. "Eliana!" he said, his voice full of anxiety. "Are you all right?"

"I . . . I want to go to the garden," she whispered.

"Fresh air will help."

He nodded. Letting her take his arm, he escorted her out the door. A cool breeze washed over them like a moonbeam over stone. Her lungs filled with the fresh evening, and the pain in her head slid away like the memory of a dream.

"I am sorry to take you away from all the fun," the oak-leaf man said, his voice so gentle and kind. "We can go back if you wish."

"Why would I give up the company of a friend in exchange for strangers?" Eliana replied. "I much prefer a friend."

He took her to the bench where the sweet-peas bloomed, and they sat and watched the stars sparkle and the moon sail through the sky. Though the stone was cool beneath them, the warmth they shared seeped into their souls. Eliana smiled behind her mask as the oak-leaf man's hand enveloped hers.

An hour was spent so, only the two of them watching the sky and listening to the distant noise of the ball inside. Suddenly the man stood up, and the icy claws of night scratched at her skin. When she reached for him, he knelt before her.

"I have a gift for you," he said.

As Eliana watched, he opened his hand. There, coiled in his palm, lay a gold chain. When he held it up, she saw that it was a necklace. Her mother's necklace.

"Where—where did you get this?" Eliana gasped, putting out her finger to touch the chain, her face full of wonder. "I thought I had lost it."

He did not answer but, leaning forward, placed the necklace around her neck, clasping it under her hair. For a moment they paused as though frozen, so close that she could feel his breath on her face. With only a fraction of movement, she might lean forward and kiss him . . . if only she had the courage!

Eliana could hardly breathe. She whispered, "I know you, don't I? I know . . ."

"Eliana," he said, his voice strained and full of some powerful emotion she hardly dared name. "Eliana, when I come to you tomorrow night, you have only to speak my name. Then I will be yours forever."

"But you've never told me your name!" she exclaimed. He moved as though to rise, and she quickly reached out, grasping at his shoulders. "Please tell me!"

He was too quick for her, however. He slipped from her grasp like running water and stood before her, his masked face lost in shadows. "I will come tomorrow night for the Reveal," he said. "In the meanwhile, try to remember."

A swift movement and a kiss on her forehead. Then the oak-leaf man was gone, a fleeting wisp of a breath. The distant church bells tolled twelve deep notes in the night.

CHAPTER
17

Lingering Threats

The following morning Martha woke Eliana with a breakfast of sweet porridge and a glass of milk to drink. When she saw that Eliana was finished and moved to take away the tray, she asked if her lady had enjoyed her second night at the ball. "Did you dance with the prince?"

Eliana frowned, her hand unconsciously straying to the gold necklace, which she had worn to bed. It lay half hidden beneath her nightgown, but she felt its contours through the thin fabric.

"Martha," she said without actually answering her maid's question, "what is Prince Ellis like?"

"Oh, very handsome, my lady!" Martha replied, eyes shining. "No taller than me I'd say, but strongly built. His hair is golden like the king's, and he has dark eyes like the queen. Such a striking young man!"

"But what is he *like?*" Eliana persisted. "Do you know anything of him personally? Is he . . . is he kind?"

"Very much so!" Martha blushed at the enthusiasm of her own words and lowered her eyes. Then, emboldened by Eliana's patient listening, she continued, "I've never met a man more gentle than he."

"You've met him then?"

"Well, you know . . . not on any *official* basis, mind you!" Her maid shook her head hastily at the silliness of this very idea. "But once I was coming up the back stair with a heavy basketful of laundry, and who do you suppose I bumped into? Prince Ellis, slipping down the back way, trying to escape his tutor! He did not see me, and we hit each other hard, scattering laundry everywhere! I scolded him roundly — then realized who he was. Oh, I thought I would die of shame!"

Eliana listened round-eyed to this story. As no more than a miller's daughter herself, she found the idea of meeting the prince under such circumstances nothing short of horrifying.

But Martha smiled at her memory. "The prince, though . . . he was such a gentleman! He apologized so prettily and helped me fetch every stitch of that laundry. 'I'm afraid it might have to be re-washed,' he said, just as though he felt bad for me. Me! Nothing but a lowly housemaid who spends her whole day scrubbing and cleaning. Then he said, 'This seems awfully heavy. Shall I carry it back down for you?'

"I tell you, my lady, I thought I might well faint, so overcome was I! Of course I told him I'm used to carrying much heavier burdens and made my escape as swiftly as I dared. But . . . well, I never forgot that one encounter." Martha's smile dimmed a little, though it remained as sweet as ever. "Sometimes I happen to see him across the way, and I'll come close to catching his eye. And I wonder if it's possible Prince Ellis remembers me as well. Though I doubt it very much! Why would he, after all?"

At this, Martha picked up the breakfast tray and hurried away, leaving Eliana to contemplate this new information. She had no way of knowing whether Martha's idealized encounter with the prince was entirely accurate or merely a romantic young house-maid's fancy. But if it was true and Ellis was a man who could speak with courtesy to a housemaid, perhaps he would not prove too difficult for Eliana to get to know.

She felt the looming dread of all those rumors once more — rumors that King Hendry intended to marry his son to Lady Gold-Spinner. To her! Twice now she had disobeyed her sovereign (albeit unintentionally) by not meeting the prince. Tonight . . . tonight, no doubt, she would meet him indeed.

And would the king insist on a betrothal?

Eliana's stomach turned at this thought. For no matter how she tried to tell herself that Prince Ellis might not make for such a bad husband . . . how could she marry him? How could she give him her hand when she knew perfectly well that her heart belonged to someone else?

Her fingers played with her mother's gold chain.

"Eliana, when I come to you tomorrow night, you have only to speak my name. Then I will be yours forever."

The memory of the oak-leaf man's urgent words pressed upon her mind. And with them another memory . . . She rubbed the chain even harder, and it warmed to her touch. The gold band about her finger warmed as well, though not so warm as to be painful. At its warming, she felt as though some icy block in her mind slowly melted away.

"To remember me by . . . to remember me by . . ."

What was she supposed to remember? A . . . a promise? But what promise —

The door to her room burst open. Eliana, still in bed, startled up with a small scream, staring into the angry face of King Hendry, who stood in the doorway.

The king — possibly a little ashamed at catching her in her bed and nightgown — did not enter the room. But he pointed one imperious finger at her, and his hand quivered with the passion of his words: "You! What do you think you are here for, you peasant girl? Do you think you can come to Craigbarr and dance and make merry without a thought?"

"Your Majesty!" Eliana cried, clutching her blankets up to her chin and wondering desperately if she should rise and curtsy.

Before she could come to a decision, Hendry continued: "You are here for *one* purpose and *one* purpose only — to marry my son!" He threw up his hands then, cursing roundly in a most un-kingly fashion. "What is wrong with you anyway? Don't you *want* to be a princess? Has all of this attention gone to your head? Do you think yourself too good for my

Ellis?"

"Your Majesty," Eliana protested, "I . . . I simply have not had opportunity to meet him—"

"*Opportunity?*" roared the king, his face going red with fury. "What have these last *two nights* been to you if not *opportunity?*" He made a desperate effort to steady himself, one hand grasping the doorpost. "Listen, girl, and listen well. Tonight you will dance with the prince. And when he asks you, you will agree to marry him. Do we understand one another?"

Eliana gazed into that beet-red face with the long, imperious mustache, the clenched jaw. She saw there the shadow of the gallows and knew suddenly, down to her very core, that the threat of death had not yet lifted from her life. This king who would kill her for not spinning straw into gold would just as happily kill her for refusing this new whim of his.

"I—I understand, Your Majesty," Eliana whispered. Her hand clenched her gold necklace hard, but it had gone cold under her touch. "I understand."

King Hendry's jaw worked as though he wanted to spew more angry words. But instead he turned away and slammed the door behind him. The whole room shook with the force of that slam. Eliana felt the reverberations down into her bones.

A sob welled up in her throat, and she struggled to choke it back down. What did it matter if the oak-leaf man came back tonight? What did it matter if she called him by name?

No one could thwart the will of a king.

CHAPTER
18

A Bargain

"Do you still think you can thwart my will?"

The faerie stood at attention on the walls of King Oberon's palace, his farseeing gaze watching the wild country for any sign of goblins. But his mind, if he was honest with himself, had been off in another world entirely — a world of mortal music and mortal dancing, where the smile of a certain mortal maiden could cause the whole universe to light up as though with purest, sunlit gold.

The roaring boom of Oberon's voice cut through this happy daydream, sending a chill of terror into the quick of the faerie captain's spirit. Still holding himself at attention, he turned and saluted, but his cheeks paled to gray.

King Oberon face was a writhing mass of storm clouds. He flew along the wall walk, trailing darkness in his wake, his fists clenched as though ready for battle. "My loyal Puck has told me all!" he declared, looming huge above his captain, for his wrath made him swell to twice his normal, towering height. "He has told me all about your sneaky doings with that mortal girl whom I *forbade* you from ever seeing again! Do you want to spend more time in my dungeons, captain? Is that your secret wish? Because I can most readily grant you this desire, and this time *I'll leave you there for a century!*"

The faerie captain was no coward, and he did not back down in the face of his king's wrath. Maintaining a most respectful tone, he offered a bow and said, "I ask forgiveness for any offense my actions have caused. But I will not ask forgiveness for the actions themselves, born as they are from the truest love any heart ever knew."

Oberon could not speak for the burning anger on his tongue. Instead, he drew back his mighty fist and would have knocked his captain clean off the wall, down onto the jagged rocks below . . .

Only suddenly, standing between him and his prey was the gloriously golden image of his wife smiling sweetly up at him.

"Really, darling, such a display. And so public too!" she said, laughing like the ringing of a bell chorus. "What will all the little ones think?"

"Out of my way, Titania!" Oberon bellowed. "Puck has told me of your part in all this nonsense, and I'll be dealing with you next!"

But Titania had seen too many of her husband's tempers over the long centuries of their marriage to mind him much now. "Don't be ridiculous," she said lightly, tapping him on the nose with one long, elegant finger. "Do you really want to stand in the way of true love? When you start meddling with people's hearts, things never go well, as *everyone* knows."

At this, some of the dark clouds in Oberon's face dispersed, giving way to a slight smile. Memory played in his mind, memory of the last time he had bested his wife in one of their battles of wills . . . memory of a donkey-headed man and a quartet of young lovers who dared run amok in his forest at night . . .

Titania, seeing that smile, knew she had scored a

point. "There now, don't you see? It's always best to let true love take its own course."

Oberon shrank back down to his ordinary height and crossed his powerful arms over his chest. "So you say, my pretty queen. But tell me . . . do you know for sure that this mortal wench is really in love with my captain?"

His gaze swiveled to the nameless faerie as he spoke. The faerie bowed again, his pale face beginning to regain color. "I do not know my dear Eliana's feelings for certain, great king," he said. "But I do have hope, indeed."

"Hope, hope!" Oberon scoffed. "What good is hope in matters of female affection?" A sly expression spread across his face, almost more terrible than his scowling wrath. "I'll tell you what, good captain and wicked queen . . . I'll make a bargain with the pair of you. Puck tells me that there is yet one night left of this mortal ball. Is this true?"

"It is true, my king," said the nameless faerie.

"And he tells me that you, my lady love, have prevented the mortal lass from meeting and dancing with the handsome mortal prince. Is this true as well?"

Titania shrugged prettily. "It was easy enough to

manage."

"So how then do we know that she would not love him, one of her own kind, better than a faerie man if given the chance?"

To this, neither Titania nor the captain could give a ready answer. Oberon laughed at the glance the two of them exchanged.

"So this is my bargain," the king said. "If you, Titania, will agree not to interfere at the ball—and by this I mean *none of your magic,* not of *any* variety—then I will let my captain attend this one last night. If his mortal lass does indeed choose him over a prince of her own kind, then I will allow him to bring the wench back here to my court." His smile was as proud and dangerous as a wild horse, and his eye gleamed with eager mischief. "Does everyone agree?"

"Most readily, my king!" answered the captain at once.

But Titania did not speak up so quickly. She eyed her husband, trying to discern what cleverness he had up his sleeve. She had played more than a few games against him in her time, and she knew better than to trust him. And the restriction upon her magic, well! That was a hard bargain indeed.

Then suddenly she began to smile to herself once more . . . such a smile as to send a hollow worry plunging in Oberon's gut.

"I agree, dearest king," she said and, standing on tiptoe, planted a kiss on his hard cheek. "I agree to your terms most heartily."

"Harrumph!" The king pushed her away, one eyebrow upraised. Addressing himself to his captain he said, "What are you waiting for then, man? Be off with you!"

The nameless faerie did not wait to be ordered twice.

CHAPTER
19

Glass Slippers

The gold-spun gown was complete.

As the team of seamstresses unrolled it on the fine rug in her bedchamber, Eliana wanted to shut her eyes. It was too much! Too rich, too gloriously gleaming! The tireless seamstress had sewn rubies and carbuncles into the sleeves and the many flounces and tucks of the skirt. The skirt opened in the front to reveal layer upon layer of frothy cream ruffles, their edges embroidered in intricate designs of flowers and birds, also done in gold thread. The fabric itself was richer, more gleaming than the finest silk — for this was faerie fabric woven of faerie thread.

And she—the miller's daughter—was expected to *wear* this?

"Let's get to work," said the head lady-in-waiting. Her sister ladies nodded, their faces grim, and they pulled Eliana into their midst. Somehow they had to make this peasant into a princess before the ball began! Eliana cast one last desperate glance over her shoulder at Martha—who offered her an encouraging smile— then succumbed to the ladies and their ministrations.

In the mayhem of strange, structured under-garments, scented bath waters, perfumes, combs, pins, stockings, and the like, no one noticed the lady in the dark hood who appeared in the corner of the room. She gazed out from underneath that hood, smiling at what she saw taking place, then looked around, searching for something, something important . . .

Ah! There they were.

Gliding like a shadow, she made her way to the little table where a pair of gold be-ribboned slippers waited to ornament the feet of the miller's daughter. They were pretty things, worthy of the fantastic gown they were designed to match.

But they were nothing compared to the pair of slippers the hooded lady pulled from beneath her cloak.

"None of *my* magic," Titania whispered even as she exchanged the glittering shoes in her hand for the golden shoes on the table. "But he said nothing of others' magic, now did he? Such a careless oversight!"

Feeling much like a proper faerie godmother from the old stories, Titania slipped away, leaving behind the work so carefully crafted at her command by the nameless captain:

A pair of delicate glass slippers sculpted from the tears of a mortal maid and a faerie man combined.

"Oh, heavens above! Where did these come from?"

Eliana, sucking in a deep breath as the ladies laced her gown as tight as some instrument of torture, turned at the sound of Martha's exclamation. She saw her maid lift two shining objects from the table.

"Put those down, girl," one of the ladies snapped with only a hasty half-glance. "They are fine shoes and . . . *Where did you get those?*" The lady dropped her hold of Eliana's laces and turned upon Martha, her sharp expression melting away in wonder at the sight of the slippers. If anything in that room could rival the beauty of the gold-spun gown, it was those two dainty objects held in Martha's work-roughened hands.

But where the dress was garish in its design, these were exquisitely simple. No adornments, no jewels or laces marred the exquisite purity of their shape. Formed of the clearest, brightest crystalline glass, they seemed to glow with some inner light.

The ladies-in-waiting clustered around Martha, leaving Eliana momentarily alone. Then they turned to her, to Lady Gold-Spinner, with wonder shining in their eyes. After all, she had, according to common knowledge, spun full rooms of straw into mounds of gold. Could she also, somehow, by her strange magic, create such beautiful things as these slippers?

They did not question her, for which Eliana was grateful. Her own mind was suddenly filled with a whirl of uncomfortable thoughts plucking and poking but not quite solidly forming. She gazed upon those shoes as Martha carried them to her, and they seemed so . . . so . . . familiar?

An image flashed across her mind's eye — the image of a man seated on a low stool, his finger held up to catch her falling tear. And that tear crystallized on the end of his finger . . .

The memory — if such it was — vanished almost

before she had time to recognize it. But this time no searing pain replaced it.

With one hand Eliana touched her mother's gold necklace draped unobtrusively about her throat, half hidden by the ruffles and jewels on the gown's bodice. With the other hand she rubbed her thumb against her mother's gold ring. Both warmed at her touch.

"Will they fit, my lady?" Martha whispered, kneeling down with the slippers before the enormous bounty of Eliana's skirts. "They seem so small."

Eliana wondered the same herself, for she did not think her feet that tiny. But, with an effort, she pulled back the ruffles and flounces and lifted a newly scrubbed and cleaned foot to Martha, who slid the slipper into place.

It fit perfectly. As did the second. Though they were made of glass and Eliana expected them to be hard and uncomfortable, she found that suddenly she could move with grace and ease, even in the vast skirts and petticoats that so imprisoned her.

"Your mask, Lady Gold-Spinner," said the head lady-in-waiting, holding out not the moon-and-sun mask Eliana had worn the previous two nights but a mask made of gold and shaped in the rays of a blazing sun.

Eliana took it uneasily. Would her oak-leaf man recognize her now? But there could be no arguing, so she slipped the mask into place.

"You are beautiful beyond words!" Martha breathed, twisting her apron in her hands with nervous delight. The ladies-in-waiting, rather than shushing the lowly maid, merely echoed her words with approving murmurs of their own. They had done their work well. Eliana, the miller's daughter, truly looked the part of a princess.

Now if she claimed the heart of the prince, she would become a princess indeed.

CHAPTER
20

Nameless

"What a glorious dress!" exclaimed King Hendry's queen. Her eyes widened hugely behind her mask and, when it seemed she could not look fully enough, she slipped the mask up onto her forehead — despite the fact that the Reveal was not due for another several hours — and openly gaped at Eliana. "Oh, it's more beautiful than I could *possibly* have imagined!"

Eliana flushed under the queen's stare . . . then paled under the king's equally potent glare. She sank into a deep curtsy, once more finding herself blessed with an unexpected grace. Ordinarily the enormous skirts would have pulled her off balance, and she would have landed in a heap of gold flounces right there on the step before her monarchs!

"Oh, darling!" the queen said without so much as acknowledging the girl. She grabbed her husband by the sleeve. "Darling, we simply *must* have my ladies make *me* a dress like that!"

"Whatever you wish, lovebird," Hendry growled. Then he reached out and took hold of Eliana's elbow, dragging her back to her feet. "All right, Lady Gold-Spinner," he said, his long mustache puffing with the force of his words, "you're not getting away so easily tonight!"

With that, he pulled her down the steps. Eliana felt the eyes of all the guests in the enormous ballroom fixed upon her. Even the musicians had stopped playing, their pipes and woodwinds dropping from their lips as they gazed up at the shimmering vision on the steps. A halo of gold light seemed to radiate from that faerie-spun dress, and the more everyone admired the gown, the more it gleamed, as though soaking in the admiration to increase its own splendor.

Eliana wished she could melt into the floor and vanish forever! Only the glass slippers on her feet gave her courage.

King Hendry, entirely unaware of the spectacle Eliana's entrance had created, focused his eye upon his son standing at the bottom of the steps. He dragged Eliana down so hastily, she would have fallen on her face were it not for the power of the slippers she wore in secret under those cumbersome skirts.

Prince Ellis, like everyone else in that room, stood transfixed by the incredible vision dragged before him. He had heard tell of Lady Gold-Spinner and her talents — heavens above, his mother had spent all this last week telling him over and over and *over* again how lucky he would be to marry this girl! — but he had never expected something like . . . like this! He couldn't even say that he had any impression of the girl herself, so lost as she was in that powerful haze of golden glory!

"Here she is," King Hendry said without preamble, and pushed Eliana right up against his son, so that Prince Ellis was obliged to take several steps back or be enveloped in vast skirts. "Girl, meet my boy. Boy, meet the gold-spinning girl. Now dance with her, devils take you! Dance!"

Prince Ellis shut his jaw with an audible *clunk*. Then, bowing with courtly courtesy, he extended a hand to Eliana. "May I have the honor of this dance,

Lady Gold-Spinner?"

Eliana cast about quickly, her eyes searching from behind her golden-sun mask for some glimpse of bronzed oak leaves. But her companion of the last two nights was nowhere to be seen. Even if he were near, how could she refuse the invitation of the prince himself? Particularly with King Hendry standing just behind her, glaring daggers into her spine.

"It . . . it would be my honor, Your Highness," Eliana whispered, and placed her fingers lightly in the prince's hand.

So she found herself led once more out into the center of the dance floor. But she felt none of the confidence and joy she had experienced while held in the arms of her oak-leaf man. She felt only terror at many, many eyes fixed so intently upon her. No one else joined her and Prince Ellis on the floor, so she could not hope to hide behind other dancers — as if it were possible to hide when clad in such a gown!

"Play!" King Hendry roared at the musicians in their gallery. They gulped and gasped and launched into a tune, hitting several sour notes until they found their stride. Prince Ellis, his eyes huge but his mouth unsmiling, began moving in the intricate paces of a dance Eliana did not know. She followed as best she could, and felt again how her crystal slippers kept her, for the most part, in rhythm with her partner.

It was nevertheless the most miserable dance she'd ever experienced.

"I have not met you at court before, have I?" the prince said, speaking with cool politeness.

Eliana glanced up at him through her sunburst mask. Did he not know her origins? Or was he simply testing her, trying to see how honest she would be? "I am a miller's daughter," she said, speaking with difficulty as she struggled to maintain the pace of the dance. "I have never been invited to court before."

She saw his eyelids flutter through the holes of his panther mask. Was it possible that she glimpsed kindness there? Could it be that Prince Ellis was as good and generous as Martha claimed he was, a man who did not scorn to speak with courtesy to housemaids or peasants?

Or was he simply embarrassed? Deeply, painfully embarrassed . . .

A sudden movement on the edge of the crowd caught Eliana's eye. She turned her head, almost against her will, and saw three figures pushing their way through the lords and ladies, three figures she knew too well! Mistress Carlyn, followed closely by Bridin and Innis. They were dressed in silks and gems but somehow managed to look drab and out of place. Where they had come by their finery, Eliana could not guess, though she suspected Mistress Carlyn had gone into deep debt with various merchants, claiming kinship with Lady Gold-Spinner and her riches.

They stared and pointed, and Mistress Carlyn waved and called out, "*Yoohoo!* Eliana dearest!"

Eliana wished she could bury herself underground and never come out again. Prince Ellis, still moving in time to the dance, looked over her head and saw the three women, saw Mistress Carlyn's rude behavior with her exaggerated gestures and smiles. "Friends of yours?" he asked, sounding as though he did not wish to hear the answer.

"My stepfamily," Eliana breathed, more ashamed than she had ever before felt in her life. By some magic she had managed to avoid even a glimpse of Mistress Carlyn and her daughters these last two nights — but apparently whatever lucky charm she had enjoyed while in the company of her oak-leaf man was now truly broken.

The song came to an end. Prince Ellis, though still holding Eliana by the hand, looked this way and that as though searching for some means of escape. Before he could settle on a course of action, Mistress Carlyn rushed out onto the floor, her two daughters trailing behind her, shamefaced with eyes downcast. There was no shame in Mistress Carlyn's face, however, as she grabbed Eliana by the arm.

"Sweetest girl!" she exclaimed, her eyes bright and cold behind her feathery mask despite the warmth of her words. "You simply *must* introduce us to this *handsome* young man!"

Eliana wanted to die. Her stepmother knew perfectly well with whom Eliana danced, and she knew perfectly well how indescribably rude it was to foist herself upon the attention of the prince himself, especially in so public a setting. There could be no excuse for this display of ill-breeding. Eliana did not even have to look at the prince to feel the enormous discomfort and irritation radiating from the very marrow of his spirit.

Though Eliana did not speak a word, Mistress Carlyn extended her hand to the prince, simpering delicately when he, after some hesitation, took it and offered the smallest bow possible. "I am Lady Gold-Spinner's mother!" she declared, then ushered her two daughters forward. "And these are her sisters, my sweet cherubs, Miss Bridin and Miss Innis." Clutching the prince's hand as though she would never let go, she swept her gaze about the watching crowd of guests and declared in a loud voice, "They are both *excellent* catches for *any* nobly born man, these *sisters* of Lady Gold-Spinner!" She addressed herself to the prince again, a secret, knowing smile creasing her painted face. "Especially now that she has caught the eye of the prince himself!"

Eliana dared cast Prince Ellis only the briefest glimpse. But in that instant she saw, even behind his mask, the deep flush of red creeping over his skin. If before he had felt only vague discomfort and disinterest in the bride his father had chosen for him, he must surely hate her now!

Ellis turned to Eliana, opening his mouth to speak words she could not begin to guess. But before he'd uttered so much as a single syllable, King Hendry's voice boomed across the way:

"Bring your lady here, my boy!"

Prince Ellis heaved a sigh but spoke no protest. He

tucked Eliana's hand into the crook of his elbow and led her away from her stepfamily, back to the grand staircase. Eliana could not say which emotion dominated in that moment—relief at leaving Mistress Carlyn behind or dread at facing the king once more.

King Hendry, with his smiling queen behind him, scowled down at the prince and the girl as they bowed and curtsied at his feet. "So you've met and you've danced," the king said, arms folded over his brilliantly embroidered jacket. "And what do you make of our Lady Gold-Spinnner, boy?"

Ellis coughed and hesitated. *Just speak the truth*, Eliana silently urged him, though she could not bring herself to so much as look his way. *Tell him you do not like me. It would be better for both of us!*

But when Prince Ellis found his voice he said, however reluctantly, "My kingly father, I have just now met the fairest maiden in all the land."

Not an ounce of truth graced his words. He said only what he knew his father wanted to hear. Eliana tried to pull her hand from his elbow, but his other hand latched down on top of hers, holding her in place.

A broad smile split Hendry's face nearly in two, almost as beaming as the smile his wife already wore.

"Excellent!" he declared. "In that case, the betrothal is set."

"No!"

A united gasp rushed through the crowd of noble onlookers. King Hendry's smile froze, and his eyes hardened behind their mask.

And Eliana, standing with her hand trapped in Prince Ellis's grasp, realized that it was she herself who had spoken.

Her breath caught in her throat . . . but she did not take back her refusal. Instead, she drew herself up as straight as she could, meeting the king's gaze through her own mask of sunbeams.

"What did you say?" the king asked, the words hissing through his mustache like snakes.

Eliana felt the delicate weight of her mother's necklace resting on her bosom. She felt the warmth of the gold ring on her finger. She gathered herself, summoning a store of courage she had not hitherto realized she possessed, and spoke in a quiet but clear voice.

"I cannot marry your son, Your Majesty," she said, "though I am grateful for the honor of his kind words. But I cannot marry him because, you see, I love another."

Another shared gasp shook the assembly like the gusting winds of a gathering storm. Someone — Eliana was quite certain it was Mistress Carlyn's voice she heard — called out in a near-hysterical voice, "Don't be a little fool!"

King Hendry stood as though transfixed before Eliana's bold words. Then he stomped down the stairs, closing the distance between himself and her, and though the mask he wore was bright and cheerful, she saw murder in his eyes.

"You have but one alternative, peasant," he whispered. His eyes promised: *I have not yet ordered my servants to tear down the gallows!*

"Come now, Father," murmured Prince Ellis reasonably. "If she loves someone else, doesn't that make for — "

"*Hsssssst!*" Hendry put up one warning hand, his gaze never breaking with Eliana's. "It's your choice," he snarled. "Your fate, your future, is entirely in your hands. So answer me now, once and for all . . . will you marry my son or won't you?"

"I will not marry him," Eliana replied.

Purple rage swept over the king's ruddy face. With a violent movement of one arm he dashed his mask from his face, then flung it to the ground and stomped it beneath his feet. "Guards!" he bellowed. "Guards!"

Eliana paled, seeing the same men-at-arms who had escorted her to and from her chamber the last three nights appear at the top of the stairs.

"Arrest this girl!" King Hendry cried, oblivious to the horrified exclamations of his queen, his son, and his many guests. "She is an imposter! She seeks to ingratiate her way into the royal household under false pretenses! She is *not* and *never will be* Lady Gold-Spinner!"

Eliana realized suddenly that Prince Ellis had dropped her arm and backed away. She stood alone in that empty space before the stairs, and the men-at-arms, looking fierce in their armor and helmets, descended upon her as if she were some dangerous enemy of the crown, not a small slip of a maiden dressed in too much gold. She retreated, her glass slippers clicking on the floor beneath her.

Then she wasn't alone anymore. Someone stood between her and the guards. Someone wearing a mask of bronzed oak leaves.

The men-at-arms paused as they reached the bottom steps, blinking hard against disbelief. Could it be true? Was it possible that this strange, tall man could manifest out of thin air right before their eyes?

"Not another step!" the oak-leaf man declared, drawing a sword from his belt, a blade which had been hidden by magic until that moment.

The guards hesitated. Then, as though coming to a joint decision, they charged, their lances aimed at the stranger's heart. But in a single smooth motion the oak-leaf man whirled, and the heads of all those lances, cut clean away, fell in a clatter upon the floor. The men-at-arms stood holding nothing more than shortened poles. One guard tried to use his as a club, but his foe kicked him hard in the stomach, sending him sprawling to his back.

The oak-leaf man turned then to Eliana and swept the mask from his face. She gazed into those brilliant green eyes and . . . and . . .

Something amazing took place!

Her mother's love, contained in physical form both in the necklace and the ring, burned bright, filling her up from the inside out. But another love blazed even brighter.

The combined tears of a mortal maid and a faerie man, mingled together in perfect purity. The tears she had shed in heartbreak—the tears he had shed in his need to mend her broken heart.

The eyes of Eliana and the nameless faerie met across that little distance between them. And each saw home in the other's gaze.

Eliana tossed her own mask aside and gathered up her golden skirts. Oblivious to all else—to the roaring of the king, to the screams of her stepmother, to the amazed voices of all the gathered crowd—she sprang forward and caught the nameless faerie by both hands. Tears fell from her eyes and from his eyes as well, and as she put her face close to his, those tears mingled and shone like the most brilliant of crystals, but full of life.

King Oberon's enchantment broke. She knew who he was.

"*Dienw*," she said, laughing through her tears. She reached up to cup his cheek in her palm. "I name you *Dienw*, for you were nameless, but now you are no longer. Thus I name you, my love, and I claim you . . . forever!"

He caught her in his arms, pressing her to his heart. Even as he did so, a powerful whirlwind spiraled down from the high ceiling above, dowsing all the candles and plunging the room into darkness. The assembled guests screamed, and many covered their faces, while others stared into the center of that maelstrom, where they saw the golden girl and her true love, holding each other close, caught up into the air itself, their hair and garments streaming.

"Seize her! Seize her!" King Hendry shouted. But it was much too late for that.

When the wind died away into no more than a whisper, the whole ballroom was as dark as a cave but for one pinpoint of brilliant light. A halo of white surrounded the perfect form of one small, gleaming glass slipper.

But Eliana and Dienw were gone.

CHAPTER 21

Home

At first Eliana was aware of nothing beyond the roaring rush in her ears and the spinning, spiraling sensation of an upward fall—a weird experience unlike anything she had ever imagined. But as frightful moments passed, she became conscious of her true love's arms around her, holding her through this tumultuous journey. She felt his heartbeat against her cheek, felt the pressure of his hands on her back. She even thought she heard his voice murmuring into the top of her head, "Hold on, Eliana. We are almost there . . ."

Then suddenly the whirlwind ceased and Eliana's feet planted on solid ground, one foot still clad in the glass slipper, one bare, so that she stood at an awkward angle.

She stood on the toes of her bare foot the next second, however, as her true love — her Dienw — caught her up and kissed her. And such a kiss it was! Full of purity and passion combined like their tears, a kiss that quite took away her breath. When he released her, she laughed then caught his face between her hands and gave him a sweet kiss of her own.

"Well, I think that will be *enough* of *that*," a thunderous voice boomed.

A spike of dread shot through Eliana's spine, and she pulled back from Dienw, whirling to face that voice, which she recognized at once. She had heard it once before, after all, back in the mortal world. Memory crashed down upon her, memory of a warlike figure bowed over her, mighty hands clutching her face. Memory of that same dreadful voice uttering a powerful faerie curse . . .

Dienw's hands caught Eliana by the upper arms and drew her against him. She took courage from his presence at her back. "My king," the faerie captain said, "this is my beloved Eliana. She has named and claimed me as her own, even as I hoped."

Eliana's blinking eyes took in her surroundings. She saw a court much grander, much larger, than any of the sights she had glimpsed at Craigbarr. And so much stranger! Chandeliers of pure crystal hung from the high ceilings, lit not by candles but by the gleaming crystals themselves. The floor at her feet was of polished marble inlaid with countless precious stones in patterns of the Hunt and the Dance and all the mad games best enjoyed by Oberon's court.

But more awful and beautiful than the surroundings themselves were the people — hundreds of strange, staring eyes in the faces of the most glorious assembly ever conceived. Some sprouted antlers from their foreheads, some antenna. Some blinked at her with faceted eyes like gemstones. They did not wear the gaudy finery Eliana had witnessed in the mortal world, for why should they ever want to? Their own beautifully proportioned limbs and exquisite faces were adornment enough, so they wore very simple robes of starlight and moonlight and moss and leaves. Eliana's shining gold gown — spun though it was by faerie magic — seemed somehow tawdry in this setting.

She wished she could turn and hide her face in Dienw's chest. And yet . . . and yet another small part of her — a part growing stronger by the minute — did not fear these people, bizarre though they may at first seem. For a secret piece of her heart responded to the sight with a faint little whisper, saying *These are* your *people, Eliana* . . .

More beautiful than all his subjects was the king himself on his high throne of antlers. He stood up now and descended the broad dais steps, his robes flowing behind him like billowing clouds. Eliana wanted to shut her eyes at the dread of his approach; but she bravely faced him, drawing strength from Dienw at her back.

"So you have won her heart," said Oberon, smiling grimly, a glint in his eye. "Well done, my captain. And I have fulfilled my part of our bargain as well and brought her here to my court."

"We shall be married at once," Dienw said. Eliana felt her heart swell with joy at the confidence of his voice.

But Oberon's smile grew and his eye glinted still more brightly. "Ah, but are you not forgetting something? Will you so easily dismiss my sacred law?"

Dienw's fingers tightened on Eliana's arms. She felt the fear that rippled through his spirit, and her own soul trembled in response, though she did not know why.

"No mortal may set foot in the Court of the Faerie King and live!" Oberon declared, flinging up his arm and pointing a long finger directly at Eliana's heart. "The penalty for such a breach is death. So this girl — this infiltrator of my world — must forfeit her life!"

Out of the shadows, dark figures moved. Figures in strange armor, holding strange weapons, closed in upon the two standing in the center of the court hall. Eliana drew a sharp breath, her heart stopping with a jarring thud against her breastbone. Dienw, quicker than thought, moved her around behind him and drew his sword once more. But he was only one against so many! Eliana had seen him fight mortals with ease, but could he fight off all of his own kind?

"No, you mustn't!" she exclaimed, catching hold of his shoulder. "I don't want you to die as well!"

Dienw shot a glance down at her, his whole heart shining in his face. "Do you think I want to live without you now?"

Before Eliana could answer, the whole of the hall rang with bright, bell-like laughter. That laughter echoed against the walls and pillars, dancing down from the ceiling itself. At first Eliana thought that the whole court had erupted into mirth at the prospect of her looming fate. But then she realized that this laugh belonged to one person only.

A great golden woman as tall as the king himself shouldered her way through the dark, warlike figures, dismissing them with little waves of her hand. "Oh, be off with you! Be off at once!" she cried merrily. "Go find some goblins to stick with those long lances!"

King Oberon folded his arms, scowling at the golden lady. "What now, woman?" he snarled. "I've honored my part of the bargain. But it's not my fault if you and my captain forgot the law in the midst of all your scheming!"

"Sweetest love," Titania cried, approaching her husband and clasping her hands theatrically over her heart. "Do you really think me such a simpleton as that? Take a moment and look at the girl properly. Look at her face! And if that is not enough to remind you, look at the necklace she wears and the ring on her finger. Look at them, husband of mine! Look at them closely."

Oberon's scowl deepened into such crevices and crags, his face was all but transformed. He turned from his wife and marched across the floor to tower over

Eliana and the captain. Dienw reluctantly stood a little to one side so as not to obstruct his master's view of the girl and her humble adornments.

The king looked. And then he stared. And then he gasped out loud, uttering a faintly spoken exclamation: "By all the Merry Dancers!"

Titania drew up beside him, taking him by the arm. "Ah! So you do remember," she purred. "You remember that chain spun from pure sunlight. You remember that band woven from pure fire. You remember those gifts you yourself gave to your sister, all those ages ago . . ."

His sister? Eliana blinked, closing her hand over the necklace upon which Oberon's gaze was fixed. "These were my mother's," she said quietly but firmly.

"Yes," Titania said, turning her magnificent smile upon Eliana for the first time. "Your faerie mother — Princess Orrla, sister of King Oberon."

Oberon blinked. There were tears in his eyes, though they did not fall. "Orrla . . . She was lost to me when she chose to abandon her own kind to marry a mortal."

"And here stands her half-mortal daughter," Titania said. "Half mortal and half faerie. And by the fey blood flowing in her veins, she is perfectly welcome here in your court!" With that she laughed again, her ringing, brilliant laugh that set the stars to dancing. She caught her kingly husband in her arms, whirling him to face her and declaring for all his court to hear, "I do believe I've won this game, sweet husband of mine!"

The king's face reddened, turning so crimson that his skin might almost have melted away. Then suddenly his laugh joined with the laughter of his wife, a deep, rolling undertone to her brightness. He kissed her soundly then declared in a loud voice, "You, my lovely tyrant, are the finest wife a man ever had . . . if simultaneously the most bothersome!"

The whole court erupted in enormous cheers. Even the dark, warlike figures threw off their shadows, shining in silver armor and pounding their lance staves upon the floor as they shouted joyous congratulations to their captain. All of those voices mingled together in a huge, echoing chorus of mirth and well-wishing.

But Eliana found her own sphere smaller and more beautiful by far, when Dienw turned her to face him, holding her hands tightly in his and gazing into her eyes.

"Dearest Eliana," he said softly, as if tasting her

name for the first time.

"Lovely Dienw," she whispered back. "I—I have no home now . . ." Pushing the words out in embarrassment, she asked, "Will you be my home?"

Mischief twinkled in the faerie captain's eyes. "With all my heart, but I will need something in return, as before. You must give me your firstborn child."

"What on earth do you mean?"

"I mean that I love you with all the love a man ever had to offer," said he. Gently kissing the back of her hand, he knelt on the marble ground, barely containing his silly grin. "I want your firstborn child to be mine. And your second, and your third, and every other child you have to be ours. Eliana, will you be my wife, my love, my home?"

"Yes, absolutely, yes!" she cried, and wrapped her arms around him, holding him close. "Of course I will, my Dienw!"

Diwedd y Stori

The wedding of the miller's daughter and the faerie captain was thrown after a faerie fashion with touches of mortal tradition. Whereas fey women wear wedding gowns of many colors, Eliana wore only white. Instead of adorning herself in many brilliant flowers, she wore a simple garland of marigolds.

She and Dienw said their vows, some in a language she did not know, then shared a kiss to seal those vows for all time. Everyone who attended their wedding could see that their love was a love that would last through the centuries.

A few days later, as Dienw escorted Eliana around

Oberon's palace, helping her to become adjusted to her new surroundings, they climbed the stairs to the tower where the crystal ball sat atop a pedestal.

"What is this?" Eliana asked her husband.

"It is for watching over the goings-on in the mortal world," he replied.

She gave him a wry smile. "You mean spying?"

"*Observing*," he answered with a grin.

"What's happening now?"

When Dienw breathed upon the surface and the crystal had fogged then cleared, it revealed down inside a scene Eliana recognized at once. It was the ballroom at Craigbarr! She realized that she was looking upon everything that happened immediately after she and Dienw escaped in the whirlwind.

"Time is different in this realm," Dienw whispered to her in explanation. "When we transported to Oberon's court, we leaped not only across leagues of land but across leagues of time as well. Though a week has gone by for us, only moments have transpired back in Craigbarr."

Eliana watched as servants scrambled to relight the chandeliers and the general panic subsided. Then Prince Ellis, his face full of fear and wonder, picked up her lost glass slipper and brought it back to the king. King Hendry, brimming with wrath at having his will so thwarted, took that slipper, held it above his head, and declared that they would search the whole kingdom over, and the maiden whose foot fit that slipper would become the prince's bride . . . like it or not!

Immediately a garish figure pushed its way through the throng. Eliana recognized her stepmother dragging Bridin and Innis in her wake. "Let them try! Let them try!" she demanded.

King Hendry, though his lip curled with distaste at the sight of the trio, could not very well back down on his word so recently spoken. So Bridin and Innis were each given a chance. Try as they would, however, Bridin's feet were too long and Innis's feet too wide. Mistress Carlyn burst into angry tears, and she and her daughters were ordered from the premises at once.

So they would return to the mill, Eliana thought, humbled and disappointed. And yet . . . and yet, perhaps Innis would marry Grahame after all. And maybe Bridin would learn at last to stand up against her overbearing mother. Though Mistress Carlyn would live on in disappointment and dissatisfaction,

Eliana hoped that her mouse-like stepsisters might find their own ways and make good lives for themselves.

Following the dismissal of Mistress Carlyn and her girls, every other eligible young lady at the ball wanted to try on the slipper. However, the glass—formed so carefully from Eliana's and her true love's tears—had been made to fit only one foot in all the worlds.

"What a shame they'll never find you!" Dienw laughed and kissed his bride. Clearly the captain did not feel sorry at all.

Eliana peered back into the crystal, her lips pursed in thought. "Could you make the slipper fit someone else?"

"I suppose. Did you have anyone in mind?"

Standing on tiptoe, Eliana whispered a name in Dienw's ear, though there was no one around to hear. He chuckled, delighted at her suggestion and, with a promise to return in a moment, vanished.

He returned soon after, panting a little, and indicated the crystal ball. "Watch now!" he urged.

Eliana stared eagerly into the crystal.

As all the noble ladies tried and failed to fit their feet into that slipper, Prince Ellis stood to one side, his expression tired and sulky. Then suddenly his face lit up with a mingling of slyness and pleasure. He called out to someone Eliana could not see.

Martha appeared on the scene, looking nervous and shaken and so small among all those fine ladies!

"Here," said Ellis, taking the slipper in his hands and kneeling before the maid. "I think you should give this a try."

"Oh, Prince Ellis!" Martha exclaimed, pressing her hand to her heart. "I wouldn't dare!"

"Nonsense," said he, with a glance at his kingly father. "You are an eligible maiden, are you not?"

So saying, he slipped Martha's work shoe off her foot and replaced it with the shining slipper.

It fit perfectly.

Prince Ellis leapt to his feet, catching Martha by the hand. "I think," he said with a winning smile that transformed his face from sulky to truly handsome, "that *you* would make a perfect princess!"

The scene faded then cleared again. Eliana, blinking back joyful tears, peered down upon the mortal marriage of the prince and the housemaid. And there stood King Hendry, looking like a man caught in a bear trap, and beside him his queen, wearing a gown of spun gold and beaming at her new daughter-in-law.

"I believe they might very well all live happily ever after," Dienw said, hugging his wife from behind and kissing her cheek. Then he laughed and shook his head. "Except for King Hendry, that is."

"Do you know?" said Eliana, taking one of his hands and pressing it in both of hers. "I think you might be right."

ABOUT THE AUTHOR

Camryn Lockhart, a college student in North Carolina, intends to pursue writing as a career. The eldest of seven, she has an Army Dad who taught her to be strong, and a Writer Mom who inspired her by reading countless books aloud and encouraging her to keep writing stories.

She has loved fairy tales since she was a little girl. Her passion is for weaving well-known tales and folklore elements into a new kind of fairy tale that retains the nostalgia of the old stories. She wants to write Christ-centered fiction that honors God. She hopes to one day write as well as C. S. Lewis and J. R. R. Tolkien, if it's not sacrilegious to hope such things.

ACKNOWLEDGEMENTS

First, I want to say how grateful I am for this amazing experience. Rooglewood Press has been wonderful through it all, and I can't thank them enough for this opportunity. I never thought I'd be a published author before I graduated from college, yet here I am!

Next, to my family, thank you for being as crazy as I am. Thank you, Dad, for working so hard to give us the childhood we had, and for helping me pursue the things I love. Thank you, Mom, for teaching me the joys of reading and writing, and for always encouraging me to keep going. Trey, my best friend and "twin" brother, thank you for our late-night talks and brainstorming sessions. I miss you so much! And thank you, Austin, Josh, Annie, Aidan, and Garrett, for being good sports when I talked over you or wanted to read something out loud. You guys are the best family I could ever ask for!

Anne Elisabeth, thank you for mentoring me and teaching me skills that have made me a better writer — an invaluable gift! I'd also like to thank John Flanagan (author of the *Ranger's Apprentice* series) who replied to my fan email when I was 13 with these words that have motivated me to write all these years: "You'll find, as you continue to write, that your characters begin to become real for you. That's when you know you've got it right."

And last but certainly not least, I thank my Lord God for giving me the gift and love for writing. He's given me so many stories to tell, and I can't wait to share them all!